ABOUT THE AUTHOR

Brian Alderson thinks that the first folk tale he can remember hearing was *The Three Bears,* and one of the first collections of folk tales that he read was a version of *The Arabian Nights.* Since that time he has told folk tales regularly to his own children, and edited several large collections, tracing some stories back to their origins.

The stories in this present book have been taken from a collection which Brian Alderson published with illustrations by Michael Foreman in 1992. It was not a hugely long book, but they tried to show how these tales were part of a long sequence told by Sheherezade over a thousand and one nights.

BRIAN ALDERSON

⟡ TALES FROM THE ⟡
ARABIAN NIGHTS

Heinemann
New Windmills

Heinemann Educational Publishers
Halley Court, Jordan Hill, Oxford OX2 8EJ
a division of Reed Educational & Professional Publishing Ltd
OXFORD   MELBOURNE   AUCKLAND
JOHANNESBURG   BLANTYRE   GABORONE
IBADAN   PORTSMOUTH (NH) USA   CHICAGO

ISBN 0 435 12447 1

First publishedin 1992 by Victor Gollancz Ltd.

First published in the New Windmill Series 1996

The moral rights of the author have been asserted

98 99 2000 10 9 8 7 6 5 4 3 2

Cover illustration by Gary Embury

Cover design by The Point

Typeset by Books Unlimited (Nottm) NG19 7QZ
Printed and bound in the United Kingdom by Clays Ltd, St Ives plc

CONTENTS

INTRODUCTION

The *Tales of the Arabian Nights* have been read and loved for centuries by people of all ages from all over the world. They are ancient folk tales linked together by one main story, and they come from the once distant lands of Persia, India and Arabia. The central story tells of the beautiful Sheherezade, who is cleverly fending off the hour of her execution by holding the Shah fascinated by her genius for telling stories. If once she loses his interest she will be beheaded.

Sheherezade's gripping tales date back to the time when all stories were told out loud and stored only in people's memories. Eventually they were written down in manuscripts, all of which told the stories in different ways. Then in 1704 a Frenchman, Antoine Galland, published some of the tales in a book and the *Tales from the Arabian Nights* became famous.

For hundreds of years these stories have been told and retold, constantly growing and changing. Brian Alderson's retelling has been based on the complete collection as translated by Sir Richard Burton, a famous Victorian explorer, who was himself embellishing an earlier translation.

Thrilling and exotic, the *Tales from the Arabian Nights* are a wonderful introduction to the rich and mysterious world of the ancient Middle East, where magic and adventure were a way of life. And what of Sheherezade? The Shah listened entranced while she told her stories for a thousand and one nights – and did she live to tell the tale?

THE TALE OF SHEHEREZADE

Once in a far off time, two brothers ruled the lands of Arabia and Persia, one to the east and one to the west. Though each saw little of the other the two brothers were very fond of one another. Both of them ruled with justice and mercy and their people loved them.

One day Shah Shahryar decided he must see his brother Shah Zaman once more. Immediately he began preparations to welcome his brother as a guest. A great caravan* bearing rich gifts was prepared and Shah Shahryar's Wazir, his chief counsellor, took the letter of invitation to Shah Zaman.

Shah Zaman accepted the invitation and also prepared a fine caravan of offerings and treasures for his brother. On the first night of the journey, however, when he was camping just outside his city walls, the Shah awoke and realized that one of the gifts, a magnificent ruby, had been left behind. He returned noiselessly to the palace and climbed up a secret stairway to his chamber. There, to his horror, he discovered his wife sleeping in the arms of a servant. Outraged, he drew his scimitar and killed them instantly. Then he took the ruby and went

* caravan: company of travellers

9

back to the camp, sick at heart from this betrayal. Even when he reached his brother's palace Shah Zaman's sorrow did not pass, and he told his brother only that he was tired.

Hoping to distract and cheer his brother Shah Shahryar organized a hunting trip, but Shah Zaman would not go, and the party left without him. Wandering from room to room of the palace Shah Zaman gazed out from a window into a secluded area of the garden. There he saw his brother's wife embracing another man. Again he was struck to the heart by the faithlessness of humankind. This time he realized that wrongdoing was not confined only to his city, and this gave him some measure of comfort.

Returning from the hunt, Shah Shahryar was delighted to see his brother in better spirits and immediately asked what had cheered him. For many days he pressed Shah Zaman to explain, and eventually his brother told him everything. Then Shah Shahryar kept watch on his wife to see if what his brother had told him was true. When he found she was indeed unfaithful, Shah Shahryar despaired. Begging his brother to go away with him from this evil place, Shah Shahryar suggested they should walk the world as poor pilgrims until they found others worse off than them.

Shah Zaman agreed, and they travelled far until they came upon someone whose experiences were more wretched even than their own. Then the brothers decided to return to the palace where Shah Shahryar ordered that his faithless wife should be put to death immediately. When his wife was dead, Shah Shahryar swore a great oath. From now on he would marry a new bride every night, and every morning he would kill her. In this way he would be avenged for the faithlessness of women.

And so it came to pass. Before long people cried out against such cruelty and hid their daughters, or sent them away lest they should become brides of the Shah Shahryar. Finally the Wazir could find no girl to bring to the Shah. The only two girls remaining in the city were the Wazir's daughters, Sheherezade and Dunyazad. However, Sheherezade was a quick-witted and intelligent girl. Though she saw how frightened her father was she refused to listen to his pleas and insisted that she would be the Shah's next bride.

The Shah himself was saddened by the news. He had known and loved Sheherezade a long time and did not wish to kill her. Even though he admired her courage he would not be seen to favour her. Orders were given for the wedding feast to be prepared, and the Shah's executioner was told to test his sharpest axe so that the bride's death in the morning would be quick.

Needless to say, Sheherezade had a plan. She told her sister Dunyazad that she would call for her in the early hours before the dawn to stay with her until her death. Dunyazad must then ask Sheherezade to tell a story to pass the time until sunrise. Sheherezade would then tell a tale so fascinating that it would save them all.

All this came to pass. Shah Shahryar, who loved a tale, agreed willingly to Sheherezade telling a story. However, the tale was so long that it took several nights in the telling. Each morning Sheherezade earned a reprieve, for the Shah could not bear to miss the end of a story. More tales were told, and more,

11

and still the Shah listened, for Sheherezade was careful to leave each story unfinished as the dawn broke.

One such story was The Tale of the Hunchback ...

THE TALE OF THE HUNCHBACK

His Lamentable Death

Once upon a time, long years ago, in a city in China there lived a hunchback who was court jester to the sultan of that place. One night he was walking through the streets when he fell in with a tailor and his wife – a jovial pair who liked any excuse for a party. So the tailor and his wife invited the hunchback home for supper and the tailor went down to the bazaar and laid in a stock of fried fish and bread and lemons and sweetmeats for dessert.

While they were feasting off these good things, the tailor's wife, by way of a joke, picked up a chunk of fish and stuffed it into the hunchback's mouth, saying:

"Now, by Allah, swallow, swallow;
If you do not, naught will follow,"

and the hunchback duly gulped it down. But the Lord looked not kindly on the joke. There was a bone stuck in the chunk of fish, which lodged in the hunchback's gullet, and without more ado he choked – and died.

Great was the consternation of the tailor and his wife. "Truly, there is no Majesty and no Might, save in Allah!" cried the man. "How should such

13

foolishness fashion such a fate?" But his wife said, "Leave thy wailing, this is what we must do. . ." and she schemed a scheme by which they would wrap the hunchback in a silken shawl and carry him to the doctor's, crying all the while that he was an infant child overcome with plague.

So this they did and the people on the streets avoided them everywhere. And when they came to the doctor's house they knocked at the door and told the slave who answered it, that they had brought a child who was sick with an unknown sickness. "Here is a silver piece," they said, "go and tell thy master to come down at once," and while the slave girl hastened off they took the hunchback into the hallway, propped him up neatly at the top of the staircase and hurried home as fast as they could.

Now the doctor was at supper with his wife, but when he saw the silver piece that the slave girl brought him he jumped up and rushed to meet the customers who were likely to prove such valuable patients; and bustling along in the dark he did not notice the hunchback's corpse leant up against the top of the stairs. He banged into it and straightway it tumbled over and rolled down to the bottom, flump!

"Lights!" he cried, "lights!" – and when the girl brought a lamp and he saw the hunchback lying there stone dead he believed that he had died from the fall. "By Hippocrates!" he said, "I have killed a hunchback," and he rushed back up the stairs to his wife, moaning and flapping his arms. "Leave thy blethering," she said, "all things can be turned to good account. We will carry him up to the terrace roof and lower him down into the dinner-man's garden, and the dogs will come down and eat him up."

For it so happened that the doctor and his wife lived next door to the reeve who had control over the Sultan's kitchen, and this reeve – whom they liked to call the dinner-man – was wont to bring home great stores of oil and fat and leftover meat and sheep's tails which he stored in his garden, where he was thus much plagued by the local rats and mice and cats and dogs, who broke in to steal the food. So the doctor and his wife carried the dead hunchback up to their open roof and then carefully lowered him down into the dinner-man's garden, where they contrived to prop him against the wall of the shed where he stored his foodstuffs.

Before long the dinner-man returned home from an evening reading of the Koran and what should he see but a shadowy figure skulking by his store-room. "Wah! By Allah," he said, "so it is men that rob me"; and he seized a hammer and knocked the hunchback on the head, clunk! At once the hunchback fell over and the dinner-man shone a lamp on him and discovered to his horror that he must have knocked him dead. "Aieee!" he cried, "a curse upon all sheep's tails and hunchbacks. Was it not enough that thou shouldst be a man of crumpled stature, and must thou be a robber too? Alas, alas, may the Veiler of all Secrets be with me in this enterprise." And he picked up the hunchback and carried him through the dark of the night to the bazaar, where he leant him against a wall as though he were a drunkard resting on his homeward way.

Soon after, along came the Sultan's steward (who was indeed drunk), and stopped by the wall to attend to some urgent business. But when he saw this figure looming beside him, he thought it to be an assassin and he straightway smote him. "Actions first, questions later," said he to himself. But no sooner had he struck the hunchback once than he toppled over and the steward fell upon him and began pummelling him and shouting for help.

This brought the watchman of the bazaar with his lamp and his cudgel, and even though the drunken steward explained the provocation he had suffered from a hunchback who sought to steal his turban and all his worldly goods, there was no doubt that the hunchback himself was dead. So the steward was taken away for trial and was condemned to be hanged that very morning.

The gallows were put up; the torch-bearer came, who was also the local hangman; the governor came to approve the execution; and a great crowd assembled to watch the fun. But no sooner was it revealed that the steward was to be hanged for killing the hunchback in the bazaar than the dinner-man came forward crying, "Stay! stay! it was not he who killed the hunchback; it was I," and he related how he had found the marauding fellow in his garden, lurking to steal his meat.

"Very well," said the governor to the torch-man, "change 'em round. Hang up this man on his own confession."

But no sooner was the dinner-man ready to be hanged than up came the doctor, crying, "Stay, stay! it was not he who killed the hunchback; it was I," and he told how he had knocked him down the staircase in his haste to lay hands on his clients' silver pieces.

"Very well," said the governor to the torch-man,

"change 'em round. Hang up this man on his own confession."

But no sooner was the doctor ready to be hanged than up came the tailor crying, "Stay! stay! it was not he who killed the hunchback; it was I," and he related the sad joke of the chunk of fish.

"Very well," said the governor to the torch-man, "change 'em round. Hang up this man on his own confession."

But by this time the torch-man on the scaffold was getting a trifle weary of all the chopping and changing and was beginning to lose interest in hanging anyone that day; while up at the court the Sultan was beginning to wonder what had become of his hunchback jester, for he'd done all his duties for the morning and wanted some amusement. So when they told him that his hunchback was down at the scaffold, stone dead, while the torch-bearer was put to a deal of trouble because so many people had claimed to have killed him, the Sultan decided he was being deprived of some curious entertainment. So he sent for his chamberlain and bade him go down to the scaffold, pay off the torch-bearer, and bring the variety of murderers before him.

What Happened at the Sultan's Court
Well –
    There's no avail
    In a twice-told tale;

so we do not need to hear again the explanations that were given to the Sultan, but when they were over he was mightily pleased and called for the whole to

17

be written in letters of liquid gold. "For," said he, "did you ever hear a more wondrous story than the four-times killing of my hunchback?"

Whether he meant the question for a statement or a challenge I do not know, but without more ado the Sultan's steward came forward:

and the Sultan's steward told what he took to be a wondrous story: a tale of a rich and handsome man who none the less stole gold for the love of a lady and lost his right hand thereby;

and he was followed by the dinner-man, who told what he took to be a wondrous story: a tale of a doctor of law, who gained entry to the harem of the Caliph Harun al-Rashid and who married its stewardess, but who lost his thumbs and his big toes because he dared to make love to her while his hands were stained from eating garlic stew;

and he was followed by the doctor, who told what he took to be a wondrous story: a strange tale of love and jealousy, whereby the son of a merchant slept with the sister of his mistress and woke to find her murdered, and how he allowed his hand to be cut off rather than confess to what had happened.

And while all these tales pleased the Sultan they seemed to him to be in no way so wondrous as the events concerning the hunchback, and it was left to the tailor to explain how, on the night when the hunchback died, he had first been to a marriage feast for one of his companions, which was attended by the guildsmen of the city:

the tailors, the silk-spinners, the carpenters and so on.

Now in the course of the feasting there arrived a young man, of most handsome appearance, except that he was lame in one leg. As he came into the company, so he observed that among the guests there was a certain swarthy barber, and no sooner had he seen him than he turned and made to leave the feast. "For," said he, "I have sworn never to sit in the same place nor tarry in the same town as this black-faced barber of ill omen."

When he was prevailed upon to speak more of this matter it came to light that he had, some time before, been in love with one of the daughters of the great judge in Baghdad. By much contrivance he had arranged to be secretly transported into her chambers while her father was at prayers, but had determined first to be barbered and had therefore sent for the silentest and peaceablest barber who could be found in Baghdad. What should be his torment, however, when a barber came who claimed to be a silent man but who, at his own estimation, was:

an astrologer,
　an alchemist,
　　a grammarian,
　　　a lexicographer,
　　　　a logician,
　　　　　a rhetorician,
　　　　　　a mathematician,
　　　　　　　an astronomer,
　　　　　　　　a theologian,

and a Master of the Traditions of the Apostle and the

Commentaries on the Koran. Not only did this Silent Barber talk so much that the young man was late for his assignation, but he was also so curious about the conduct of the affair that he caused mayhem round the house of the great judge, with the result that the young man was tipped out of a window and broke his leg. So who should wonder that, through losing his lady and losing his limberness, he should never wish to see the barber again.

For his part, however, the barber gave token of the truth of all that the young man said, first by telling the assembled company at the marriage feast of his fame as a Silent Man and then by embarking upon six inconsequential tales, one for each of his brothers: the Prattler, the Babbler, the Gabbler, the Long-necked Gugglet, the Whiffler, and the Man of Many Clamours – as a result of which the tailor and his friends locked the barber in a cupboard and there let him rest till his tongue should have cooled down.

"In sooth," cried the Sultan, "I should like to see this barber," and straightway he was sent for and released from his cupboard and came before the Sultan, where were also to be found the tailor and the doctor and the dinner-man and the steward and the corpse of the hunchback. They explained to him how this audience had come into being to hear his adventures, but before he could ever begin, he looked round the faces of them all and then laughed till he fell over backwards.

"Truly," he said, "there is a wonder in every death, but the death of this hunchback is indeed worthy to be written in letters of liquid gold!" And he went over to where the corpse was lying and took from his barber's bag a little pot of ointment, with which he anointed the hunchback's throat, then he drew out the chunk of fish with its bone, all soaked in blood. Thereupon the hunchback sneezed, like one who has eaten raw horse-radish, and jumped up as if nothing had happened.

From that day forth he continued to jest before the Sultan, just as the tailor tailored, the doctor doctored, the dinner-man dined, the steward stewed and the barber barbered until there came to them all, each in his turn, the Destroyer of Delights and the Sunderer of Societies.

And when Sheherezade had completed the Tale of the Hunchback she went on to tell more tales of the kings and princes of the land. She told too, out of her recollection, fables of the birds and beasts, among which was:-

THE FABLE OF THE BIRDS AND THE BEASTS AND THE CARPENTER

In times of yore a peacock lived with his wife on a piece of land beside the sea. But the place was infested with lions and all manner of wild beasts so the two birds sought for some other abode and eventually happened upon an island, verdant with trees and fresh with running streams.

Now while the birds were enjoying the fruits and the waters of their new home there came before them a duck, flapping its wings and crying in terror, "Beware, and again I say beware, of the Sons of Adam!" But the peacocks spoke comfortingly to the duck, saying that they would defend her against all creatures, and that anyway there could be no Sons of Adam upon this island.

"Alhamdohlillah!" cried the duck, "glory to God for your kindness, but you must know that the Sons of Adam have learned how to traverse the waters of the sea and that there is none like them for mischief and crafty cunning." And the duck went on to relate how one day she had been warned in a dream to flee the Sons of Adam and how in her wanderings she had come upon the whelp* of a lion sitting at the door of a cave.

* whelp: cub

"Draw near," called the lion, "and tell me thy name and nature."

"My name is Duck, and I am of the bird-kind; and what of thee?"

"My name is Lion. My father hath warned me against those creatures named the Sons of Adam and I am seeking them across the world that I may kill them."

So Duck was glad to travel under the protection of Lion, and they had not gone very far before they saw a cloud of dust approaching them. As it came near they perceived at its centre a running naked ass, tearing across the land.

"Hark ye, crack-brain!" called Lion. "What is thy name and nature?"

"O Son of the Sultan, I am Ass and I am fleeing a Son of Adam."

"Whyso? Dost thou fear he will kill thee?"

"Nay, O Son of the Sultan, but I fear his cheating ways, for he hath a thing called a Pack-saddle which he setteth on my back, and a thing called Girths which he bindeth about my belly, and a thing called a Crupper which he putteth beneath my tail, and a thing called a Bit which he placeth in my mouth; and he fashioneth a Goad to drive me to do his bidding and carry his wares. And when I can work no more he will kill me and cast me on the rubbish heap for dogs."

"Fear not," said the lion whelp, "for Duck and I will defend thee," and they continued on their way. They had not gone far before they saw another cloud of dust approaching them across the plain, and this proved to be a black horse with a silver blaze on his forehead.

"Come hither, majestic beast," called Lion, "and tell us thy name and nature."

"I am Horse of the horse-kind and I am fleeing a Son of Adam."

"Whyso? How should so mighty a creature as thyself be afraid of a Son of Adam when one such as I is seeking only to meet and slay him? Surely one kick from one of thy hoofs would prevail against him?"

"Nay, O Prince," said Horse, "do not be deluded; for he hath a thing called a Hobble which shall prevent me from doing so, and when he is minded to ride me he hath a Saddle and Girths and a Bit and a Rein with which to make me do his bidding. Then when I grow old and can no longer run for him he will sell me to the miller to grind corn and the miller, in his turn, will sell me to the knacker, who will cut my throat and flay my hide, and pluck out my tail for the sieve-maker, and boil my fat for tallow candles."

When the lion whelp heard these words his rage against this Son of Adam increased and he sought directions from Horse where they might find the creature; and before they had gone far they encountered a furious camel, gurgling and pawing the earth with his feet. This mighty beast the lion whelp took to be a Son of Adam, but before he could spring at him and tear him to pieces Duck explained that his name was Camel, and Camel explained that he was himself fleeing from a Son of Adam.

"Whyso? Surely with one kick of thy hoof thou wouldst slay him?"

"Nay, O Prince," said Camel, "for he is a creature of wily ways and he putteth into my nostrils a twine of goat's hair called a Nose-ring, and over my head a thing called a Halter and he delivers me to the least of his children to lead about the world; and when I am old and good for nothing he selleth me to the knacker who cuts my throat and makes over my hide to the tanners* and my flesh to the cooks."

"Where didst thou leave this Son of Adam?" asked the lion whelp.

"Why, even now he cometh after me and I am away now to the wilds where he will not find me."

"Nay, O Camel, stay with us and thou wilt see how I shall tear him to pieces and crunch his bones and drink his blood … "

And as Lion was speaking there came towards them a little, old, bent, lean man, carrying on his shoulders a basket of carpenter's tools and on his head a branch of a tree and eight planks. When Lion saw him he walked towards him and the man smiled at him and said: "O King, who defendeth these creatures from harm, Allah prosper thy ways and strengthen thee, that thou mayst protect me too!"

"Whyso? What is thy name and nature – for assuredly thou art a beast the like of which I have never seen before and I would wish to aid thee, if only for the eloquence of thy words."

"O Lord of wild beasts, I am a carpenter, and I am journeying to thy father's Wazir, the lynx, to make for him a shelter against the Sons of Adam. For he knows the ways of those creatures and he would have a house wherein he might dwell and fend off his enemies."

Now when he heard this the lion whelp grew envious of the lynx and he said to the carpenter, "By

* tanners: leather workers

my life, I will have you make a house for me with those planks before ever you go to Sir Lynx."

"O Lord of wild beasts," said the carpenter, "that may not be. I will go first to the lynx and then return to thy service and build thee a house."

"By Allah," roared the Lion, "thou shalt not leave this place till thou build me a house of planks!" and he sprang at the carpenter so that he fell over and his gear fell to the ground. "Yea; thou mayst in truth fear the sons of Adam, O Carpenter, for thou art a feeble beast with no force to protect thee."

But the carpenter got up and smiled at Lion, saying, "Well, I will make for thee a house." And he took his planks and nailed together a dwelling in the form of a chest after the measure of a young lion. And he left one end free for a door and he took hammer and nails and said to Lion, "Enter the house through this opening, that I may fit it to thy measure."

So the whelp rejoiced that he had his way and crept through the opening into the house. Once he was inside, the carpenter whipped the lid on to the opening and nailed it down.

"O Carpenter," cried Lion, "what is this narrow house thou hast made for me? Open the gate and let me out!"

"Alas!" said the carpenter, "I am but feeble and lacking in force and I know not what may befall me if I release you once more among these creatures here. Perhaps I shall send for the lynx, that he may inspect my capabilities as a builder of houses."

And with that Ass and Horse and Camel – and even Duck – knew that this was a Son of Adam and they took their ways in haste less the carpenter should build dwellings for them too.

And after telling that fable Sheherezade went on to tell how there are indeed no limits to greed and betrayal. Firstly she told:-

THE FABLE OF THE WOLF AND THE FOX

Some time ago a wolf and a fox set up house together. But the wolf was forever tyrannizing the fox, putting him in his place like a servant, buffeting him, and doing down all his offers of friendship. The fox smiled through it all though, but in his heart he said, "There is no help for it; I must encompass the destruction of this wolf."

Now one day the fox came upon a vineyard, and as he walked round it he saw a hole made in part of its wall. But experience had taught him to be wary of such pretty invitations and he crept carefully up to the hole and looked at it closely. And indeed it was a trap, for the owner of the vineyard had dug a deep pit beyond it, lightly covered with a mat of sticks, to catch whatever wild beasts were foolhardy enough to come in to the vineyard through the hole.

So the fox said to himself:

"To refrain
Is to gain –

Praise be to Allah that I was so cautious; but let me see what my friend the wolf thinks of this."

So the fox returned home and said to the wolf, "Allah hath made plain for thee a way into the vineyard."

"How should that be?" said the wolf, "how can such a one as thou know such a thing?"

"Why," said the fox, "I went to the vineyard myself. I saw that the owner was dead (torn to pieces by wolves, so they say) and there was the fruit shining amongst the vines."

The wolf doubted not so precise a report as this and his gluttony was aroused and he set off for the vineyard, with the fox not far behind him.

"There," said the fox, directing him to the fallen wall, "thou mayst enter without the trouble of climbing a ladder," and the wolf jumped and fell straight into the pit.

At this the fox sat back on his haunches and laughed with his chops wide open and his tongue hanging out. But before long he heard the wolf in the pit lamenting and crying, so he, too, put on a sad, tearful face and looked over the side of the hole. "Why, Friend Fox," said the wolf, "I see that thou, too, art saddened by this dismal fate that has befallen me – but can we not devise a means by which I may escape this pit?"

"Nay, nay, Friend Wolf," said the fox, "do not misunderstand me. I do not weep for thy plight, but for all the long life that has passed, when thou demeaned me and smote me; and I weep that thou didst not fall into this pit months ago." And with that the wolf and the fox fell to arguing over their past life together, and eventually it seemed that the wolf repented. "In truth," he said, "I have woefully wronged thee, but if Allah deliver me from this pit I will assuredly reform my ways, take on the mantle of holiness, and go upon the mountains like a pilgrim praising Him."

At these humble words the fox took pity on the wolf and, coming up to the pit, he turned and dangled his tail over the edge so that the wolf might seize it and drag himself out. But no sooner had he done so than the wolf gave one big tug to his tail and pulled him into the pit as well. "So-ho!" he said, "thou fox of little mercy, one minute thou art up there laughing at me, and the next thou art down here once more under my dominion. Assuredly I will hasten to slay thee before thou seest me slain."

"Aha!" said the fox to himself, "now am I indeed fallen back into the snare of the tyrant and I must use all my craft and cunning to escape this foe." And forthwith he began to argue with the wolf, saying that he had offered help only because the wolf had repented and turned to Allah and that it would do his case no good if they both were to die in the pit, but that they might yet both be saved. "If thou stand up at thy full height," he said, "and I climb on thy back so that I come near the top of the hole, then may I spring and reach the ground and fetch the wherewithal to rescue thee."

The wolf placed no trust in this plan, but he perceived that there might be no other way of getting out of the pit, so he permitted the fox to mount his shoulders, raised himself up to his full height, and the fox jumped out of the pit like a chestnut jumping out of the fire. "O double-deceiver," he cried to the wolf, "make sure of thy repentance and call truly to Allah, for I will never trust thee again."

And at that he climbed on the wall overlooking the vineyard and cried to the men working among the vines that a wolf was fallen into the pit. And as all the men came running with sticks and stones to slay the wolf, the fox walked quietly down to the vineyard and ate up all the grapes.

And then Sheherezade went on to tell:-

THE FABLE OF THE MONGOOSE
AND THE MOUSE

Once upon a time there lived together in the house of an old farmer a mongoose and a mouse, sharing whatever food they might come by. Now it so happened that the farmer fell sick and the village doctor ordered that he should be given a diet of sesame seeds with the husks taken off. So the farmer's wife sought a measure of sesame from her neighbours and she steeped it in water, took off the husks and spread it out to dry; then she went about her tasks in the fields.

Well, the mongoose observed these goings-on, which seemed to him like the preparation of a banquet for mongooses, and when the farmer's wife went out he came in and began to carry off the husked sesame to his dwelling behind the wall. He laboured at the work all day, and by the evening, when the farmer's wife came back, she found only a few seeds left on the table.

"By Allah!" she said, "there is a thief at work," and she sat down with a cudgel and watched.

After a time the mongoose came out of his hole to bring in all that remained for his feast. However, he perceived the farmer's wife with her cudgel and he said to himself, "So-ho, this lady may be after taking the skins off more than sesame seeds. It behoves me

32

to be prudent", and he straightway returned to his hole and began to carry forth the seeds that he had already collected and lay them back among the rest.

"Forsooth," said the farmer's wife, "this creature cannot be the cause of our loss for he brings the sesame back from the hole of him who stole it. Kindness must surely be the reward of kindness." And she held her hand and continued to sit and watch.

Now the mongoose guessed what she might be thinking and when he saw his companion the mouse, he said, "O my sister, I should not be a good neighbour to you if I did not tell you that our hosts out there, the farmer and his wife, have brought home a feast of sesame. They have eaten their fill of it, and now there are leavings fit for the king and queen of the mice, strewn all over the table."

So, squeaking for joy, the mouse ran from her hole and frisked and frolicked amongst the grain which the mongoose had so diligently returned to the table.

And when the farmer's wife saw this she deduced that here was the culprit and she smote the mouse with her cudgel, bonk!

From that day forth the mongoose lived a life of ease and contentment, cared for by the farmer's wife and not sharing a morsel with anyone.

When these fables were told Sheherezade went on to relate to the Shah Shahryar many extravagant stories of the kings and caliphs of Arabia.

There was, for instance:

The Pathetic Tale of Ali bin Bakkar and Shams al-Nahar and their unrequited love;

The Fantastic Tale of Kamar al-Zaman who chose

never to wed mortal woman but changed his mind when the spirits of the air brought to him, as though in a dream, the Princess Budur, who had chosen never to wed a mortal man; and

The Strange Tale of Mohammed bin Ali, the jeweller, who pretended to be the Caliph of Baghdad out of frustrated love for the Lady Dunya, the sister of the Caliph's Wazir.

When these fables were told Sheherezade went on to tell the Shah Shahryar many stories about the kings and rulers of Arabia and after these tales Sheherezade told:-

THE TALE OF THE EBONY HORSE

His Coming

In times gone by there lived a great and generous
Emperor of the Persians and he had one son and
three daughters – all as radiant as the full moon.

Every year the Emperor was accustomed to hold
two festivals, at the time of the New Year and at the
Autumn Equinox*, when his palace would be open to
all who cared to enter and when there would be
much rejoicing and giving of gifts. And so it came
about that one year three sages came questing to the
palace, bringing curious presents by which they
hoped to obtain betrothal to the Emperor's three
daughters.

The first sage, who was from India, laid before the
Emperor the carved figure of a man, inlaid with
jewels and bearing a golden trumpet. "What then is
the virtue of this gift?" asked the Emperor, and the
Indian sage explained that the figure had only to be
set up at the gate of the city for it to be guardian over
all. "If an enemy approaches," said the sage, "it will
blow a blast on this clarion-trumpet and he will be
seized of a palsy and drop down dead." So the
trumpeter was set up at the gate and the sage was

* equinox: when day and night are the same length

35

granted the hand of the Emperor's eldest daughter in marriage.

The second sage, who was from Greece, laid before the Emperor a basin of silver in whose midst was fashioned a peacock and twenty-four chicks all of beaten gold. "What then is the virtue of this gift?" asked the Emperor, and the Grecian sage explained that for every hour that passed of the day or night, the peacock would cry and peck one of its twenty-four chicks and flap its wings, and then at the end of the month it would open its beak so that the new crescent moon could be seen inside. And even as he spoke, an hour struck and the peacock cried and pecked and flapped its wings, so the Emperor was well pleased and granted the sage the hand of his second daughter in marriage.

Then there stepped forward the third sage, who was a Persian necromancer, an old man an hundred years old, with white hair and a face like a cobbler's apron: sunken forehead, mangy eyebrows, red goggle eyes, pendulous* lips and a nose like a big black aubergine. His gift to the Emperor was a horse, fashioned full-size out of ebony, inlaid with gold and jewels, and harnessed up with saddle, bridle and stirrups. "What then is the virtue of this gift?" asked the Emperor, and the sage replied that one had only to mount the horse and prepare oneself aright, to be able to fly through the air and cover the space of a year in a single day. So the Emperor thanked the Persian magician and granted him the hand of his youngest daughter in marriage.

* pendulous: drooping

36

Now it so happened that the Emperor's daughters had been hiding behind a curtain to watch all these proceedings and when the youngest daughter perceived who her husband was to be, she fled to her chamber and began weeping and wailing and tearing at her hair and her garments. This racket came to the ears of her brother, Kamar al-Akmar, the Moon of Moons, who had just returned from hunting, and he went up to her room and asked her the cause of her distress. "O my brother," she cried, "know that there has come to court this festival day a dreadful magician, with a face like the Jinni who frightens the poultry in the hen-houses; he has given to our father as a gift a horse made of black wood, to which our father has returned him a promise that he may have my hand in marriage. Alas, that I should ever have been born."

When her brother heard this, he soothed her as best he could and made his way to the Emperor and said, "Who is this wizard with a face like an ill-made pot who hath bewitched thee into giving away my sister? What is this gift of his that has brought her to such misery?" So the Emperor told him of the visit of the sages and sent servants to fetch the ebony horse and show it to him, little knowing that the Persian wizard had been standing nearby, had heard everything and was filled with mortification and anger.

So when the servants brought the ebony horse and the Prince mounted it to try its virtues, the sage stepped forward as though to instruct him. "Trill* this," he said, pointing to a pin on the side of the

* trill: to twist

horse's head, and the Prince had no sooner turned it than the ebony horse seemed to take breath and soared off into the air, with the Prince sitting astride its back.

"Very well," said the Emperor, "but tell me, O sage, how may he turn the horse and how make it descend?"

"Alas, my lord," said the sage, "I can do nothing, and we may never see him again till Resurrection-day, for he was so proud and eager to be off that he did not stay to ask me what mechanism he might use to bring the creature back to the ground." And the magician smiled grimly, for he had so contrived it to be revenged upon the Prince for seeking to thwart his marriage. But the Emperor was himself angry and he ordered that the sorcerer be at once clapped into jail and there bastinadoed on the soles of his feet.

What Happened to the Prince

When he felt the ebony horse move under him and then rise in the air, the Prince was filled with great joy. Never in his years of hunting had he travelled so fast or seen so far as now. But as the horse made unswervingly towards the sun the Prince became troubled in his mind as to how he might turn the beast round, let alone bring it down. "Verily," he said to himself, "this is a device of the sage to destroy me for championing my sister."

For a huntsman, though, he was not without wit, and he fell to examining the carcass of his horse in the belief that one pin for setting off might be matched by another pin for setting down and, behold! beneath the carved shoulders

38

of the horse he found what seemed to be two ornamental cocks' heads, and as he twisted one, so he was able to steer the horse and as he twisted the other, so he was able to bring it into a gradual descent. Thus he passed over mountains and deserts, oceans and forests, even to the boundaries of China.

By this time the day was waning and he determined to find somewhere he might pass the night, and he saw below him a fine city with, in its centre, the towers and battlements of a majestic castle. "This is a goodly place," he said to himself, and he turned the pin to descend and the horse sank down with him like a weary bird and alighted gently on the terrace roof of the castle.

"Alhamdohlillah," said the Prince, "praise be to Allah for my safe journeying," and since, by now, the night had fallen he set off through the sleeping palace to see if he might find food and water for himself. First he came to a staircase which took him down to a courtyard paved with white marble and alabaster, shining in the light of the moon; then he traversed chambers and passage-ways, all unguarded and empty, until eventually he came upon the entrance to the harem, at whose door slept a giant eunuch as though he were a tribesman of the Jinn, longer than lumber and broader than a bench. Beside him was his sword, whose pommel gleamed in the candle flames, and above his head on a column of granite there hung a leather bag.

Praying again to Allah, the Prince carefully lifted down the bag and found within it a great store of provisions with which he refreshed himself. He then replaced the bag and, taking the eunuch's sword, he crept forward to where Destiny should take him.

Beyond the door of the harem there was a second door, with a curtain before it. This he raised and beyond it he saw a couch of white ivory, inlaid with pearls. Slave girls were sleeping at its corners and upon the couch itself there slept a lady, beautiful as the moon, and robed only in her hair. The Prince was overcome by her loveliness and, caring nothing for discovery or death, he went up to her and kissed her on the cheek. At once she awoke, opened her eyes and said, "Who art thou and whence camest thou?" to which the Prince replied, "I am thy slave and thy lover."

"But who brought thee hither?"

"My Lord and my fortune."

Now it so happened that only the day before, the lady's father, who was King of that land, had had audience of the King of Hind who sought to marry her; now the King of Hind was ugly and uncouth and had been sent away, but the lady believed that our Prince was he and she deemed it most blameworthy that she should be denied one so handsome. So she set about shouting with anguish, at which her slave girls all woke up and before long the palace was in uproar. The slave girls woke up the eunuch; the eunuch, missing his sword, believed that bandits had come to the palace and rushed to wake the King; the King called up his household guard and everyone ran pell-mell to the Princess's bedroom, where she continued to wail that she had been cheated of her lover, and where the Prince Kamar al-Akmar was lost in wonder at all the hubbub.

Eventually the eunuch explained to the King that

he thought vandals had stolen his sword, and the slave girls explained to the eunuch that he had allowed a man to enter the harem, and the Princess explained to the slave girls that she wanted to marry the Prince, whether he came from Hind or no, and the Prince politely said to all and sundry that he would be glad to sign the marriage-contract as soon as it was indited*.

None of this could assuage the wrath of the King, though, who did not care for a stranger to make himself so free with his daughter before ever he had been introduced. "How can we know," he cried, "that thou art an Emperor's son as thou sayst? What Emperor shall save thee if I call upon my slaves and servants to put thee to the vilest of deaths?" To which the Prince replied that he would be pleased to stand in single combat for his honour against the King himself or else stand against the King's whole army to gain his daughter's hand.

Well, the King had no liking for single combat against one so doughty as this strange prince, so it was agreed that next morning he should confront the King's whole army, and that was forty thousand horsemen and a like number of slaves and followers. "This Prince, for his honour," cried the King when all were assembled, "this Prince pretendeth that he can overcome you in combat to gain the hand of my daughter and that, were you an hundred thousand, he would force you to flight, so when he comes upon you, show him that he has chosen a mighty task." Then, turning to the Prince, he said, "Up, my son, and slaughter my army."

* indited: written

But the Prince turned to the King and said, "My Lord, how shall I come against this host without any horse?" To which the King gave answer that he might chose any mount from the King's own stables. "But not one of those horses pleaseth me," said the Prince, "I will ride none other but the horse on which I came."

"Then where is thy horse?" asked the King.

"Atop thy palace," answered the Prince.

"Where in my palace?" asked the King.

"On the roof," answered the Prince – and with those words it seemed to the King that this comely, daring fellow was indeed mad.

"How can a horse be on the roof!" he cried; but he forthwith sent servants back to the palace with instructions to bring back whatever they might find on the roof and before long they returned bearing the ebony horse, which, gallant as it looked (and though it was indeed on the roof), hardly seemed a fit charger to accost the King's whole army. "Is this then thy horse?" asked the King.

"Yes, O King, this is my horse; and if thou wilt bid thy troops retreat as far as an arrow can fly from it then I will mount and charge."

So the troops withdrew and the Prince climbed into the saddle and forthwith trilled the pin of ascent; and as everyone watched to see him charge, the horse began to rock and sway as though it were taking great breaths, and then it rose in the air and flew off over the heads of the waiting troops. "Catch him! Catch him!" cried the King; but his Wazirs and ministers replied, "Oh who can overtake a flying bird?" and as the Prince fled away in the sky, the army was left to return to quarters and the King's daughter relapsed into tears and grief.

"By Allah!" she cried, "I will neither eat nor drink nor sleep till Allah return him to me."

The Homecoming of the Ebony Horse
Once the Prince had contrived his flight from the King he set his horse's head in the direction of his homeland and before nightfall he was again in the palace of his father. But how changed everything was. For now, instead of the bright traffic of the festival day, all was still and shrouded, with black hangings on the walls and ashes strewn upon the floor; and when he made his way to the Emperor's chamber he found his father and mother and his sisters clad in the black robes of mourning and pale with grief.

When he entered the room though, they started up in surprise for it was his supposed death that they had been mourning, and before long they were clambering over him, hugging and kissing him and shouting for joy. The Emperor ordered a great banquet to be prepared and a holiday was proclaimed throughout the land. Streets and markets were hung with garlands, drums and cymbals were beaten, and a general pardon was given to all who were imprisoned (including, not least, the Persian necromancer, who was rewarded with robes and honour now that the ebony horse had returned, but of whose marriage to the King's youngest daughter nothing more was said).

Amid all the merriment, however, the Prince felt little but sadness and longing for the Princess that he had left behind so far away. He confessed his love to his father, the Emperor, saying that he was determined once more to mount his ebony horse and ride to find her, and his father gave his consent – although privately he wished to make nothing more than a bonfire of the horse and its tricks.

So the Prince rode once more into the sky and made his way to that palace roof where he had alighted so few days ago. He made his way quietly to the harem, finding the eunuch asleep as usual; but when he came to the Princess's chamber there was little need for quietness since she was still wailing and bawling over the loss of the Prince who had flown away. As soon as she saw him, however, she was struck dumb with wonder, and when he suggested that she might this time ride back with him to his father's kingdom she was overwhelmed with joy. She dressed herself in the richest of her dresses, furnished herself with all manner of gold ornaments and jewels, and the Prince then carried her up to the terrace roof where the ebony horse patiently waited. They climbed on its back and the Prince secured the Princess to him with bonds of silk, twisted the pin to ascend and away they flew over forests and oceans, deserts and mountains, back to the land of Persia.

When the city of the Emperor came in sight, the Prince determined that he would take his bride to one of the pavilions in the Emperor's garden where she might rest awhile, before he summoned his father and the royal court to greet her. Accordingly, he caused the horse to alight in a secluded corner of the grounds and there he left the Princess, seated in a summer-house, while he went to announce their arrival. "Rest here," he said, "and watch over our horse, until I, or my messenger, come to thee to bring thee an Emperor's welcome to this land," and he forthwith betook himself to the palace to give tidings of their coming to his father and his family.

Great was the joy at his return. The Emperor straightway ordered a continuance of the general rejoicing and prepared a great train of courtiers and ministers, members of the royal household, slaves and eunuchs to go to make welcome the Princess. He himself led the procession and to the music of drums and trumpets they made their way across the gardens to the summer-house.

But when they arrived, they discovered with dismay and consternation that no one was there. The Princess and the ebony horse had gone.

What Happened to the Princess

Now it so chanced that when the Prince brought the ebony horse to rest in his father's demesne* he was observed by the Persian necromancer who was in the garden seeking herbs and simples* for his cauldron. With great caution, therefore, he slunk over to the pavilion and overheard the last of the Prince's conversation with his bride.

Allowing a suitable amount of time to elapse, the wizard then made his way to the Princess, bowed down before her and kissed the ground between his hands. "And who art thou?" asked the Princess, not a little alarmed at the sudden appearance of a man of such monstrous ugliness.

"O my lady," said the wizard, "I come from the

* demesne: territory   *simples: medicinal herbs

45

Prince, who hath bidden me to conduct thee to the palace of his father."

"Why came he not himself? And could he not find a messenger more handsome for this joyous occasion?"

"Ah, my lady," said the wizard, "he is even now preparing a royal greeting for thee; while as to myself, is it not fitting that so bright a jewel as thou art, should be set off against so plain an attendant as I?"

"Very well," she said, "then let us go forward to the Prince. But what hast thou brought for me to ride?"

"O my lady, thou mayst ride the horse that thou camest on."

"But I cannot ride it myself."

"Then I must needs accompany thee," said the magician, and he mounted the ebony horse, took the Princess up behind him, and after binding her securely in her seat he trilled the ascent-pin and the horse gathered itself and rose into the air. Away it went, beyond the confines of the palace, beyond the city – over the hills and far away.

"Ho thou," cried the Princess, "where goest thou? Where is the Prince?"

"Allah damn the Prince," cried the magician, "he is a mean, skinflint knave!"

"Then woe to thee, that thou disobeyest thy Lord's commandment!"

"He is no Lord of mine, but rather my enemy. For thou must know that I am the creator and master of this horse, which he took from me by a stratagem*,

* stratagem: trick, plot

and now that I have it again I shall never relinquish it. Thou and I shall fare forward into a new life of power and riches." And he turned the horse's head towards the west and ceased not to ride till they reached the land of the Greeks where he brought them all to rest in a green meadow by a stream.

Now this meadow lay close to the city of a great Grecian King, who at that time was walking nearby in the cool of the evening. When he saw this strange pair with their wooden horse, the rough-visaged Persian and the comely lady, he deemed some mystery was afoot and he sent his slaves to take them and bring them to audience at his royal palace.

"Who art thou?" he asked, "and whence comest thou with thy toy horse?"

"We are of Persia," said the magician, "way-worn travellers, man and wife." But the lady would not hear of such a thing. "O King," she cried, "that is not so. He is naught but a wicked necromancer who has stolen me away by force and fraud..." and she prostrated herself before the King.

Well, there seemed little doubt as to the truth of her denunciations, and the Grecian King ordered the sage to be taken to prison and there (again) bastinadoed. The mysterious horse he placed within his treasure-house, and the lady within his harem where she fell weeping and wailing so that none could come near her.

And How it All Ended
Now when the Prince Kamar al-Akmar discovered the summer-house empty in the garden, with horse and Princess gone, he realized that their disappearance could only be the work of the Persian

47

necromancer, for he alone knew the secret mechanisms of the horse's flight. So the Prince bade farewell to his father and his family and set out into the world to find the villain.

He travelled through many lands, inquiring if people had heard tell of a strange horse of ebony that flew down out of the sky – but apart from suggestions made about the state of his own wits he was told nothing. Then one day, arriving at a certain khan, he came upon some merchants talking and overheard one of them tell how in such-and-such a city in Greece the King had come upon an ill-assorted couple – a foul-visaged Persian and a beautiful maiden – standing beside a wooden horse which they seemed to have carried to the middle of a field but could carry no further.

At once the Prince besought the merchant for a closer account of what he had heard, and when he had ascertained the name and region of the city he turned his steps towards that part of Greece and did not rest until he was outside its walls. When he arrived, though, it was evening and he was taken into the gatehouse to be questioned and to be held for the night. "Where are you from?" they asked.

"I am a Persian from Persia," he replied, at which the guardsmen fell back with laughter (for in those days the Persians were deemed great liars and the Greeks had a joke about one of them who said, "I am a Persian, but I am not lying now"). "Ho, ho," said the guard, "well let's hope that that is not so great a lie as the ones we have been hearing from that other Persian traveller who even now is taking his ease in our prison." And he went on to tell the story of the King's discovery of the magician and the Princess, how the one kept speaking of a horse that flew through the air and how the other was in a fit of madness, wailing and raving, so that never a doctor could get near to cure her – for the King had fallen madly in love with her and was seeking physicians from all quarters of the earth who might mend her wits.

From these words the Prince gained some notion of how he might proceed in his plan to rescue the Princess, and the next morning, when he was brought before the King, he put out that he was a travelling doctor come to try to cure the Princess's madness. So the King had him taken to the chamber where the Princess was kept and there he found her, not possessed of any evil Jinn, but writhing and wringing her hands that none might approach her.

When the Prince saw her thus he bade her attendants leave the room and he stepped towards her saying, "No harm shall betide thee, O ravishment of the three worlds"; and when she perceived who spoke she fell down as though in a swoon. Then the Prince went up to her and whispered to her to be calm and patient. She was now to pretend to be cured and was to speak kindly to the King who sought her love, and if Allah willed then they would reach an end of their tribulations.

Then the Prince returned to the King and bade him go in to the woman, for he had taken away her madness. "But beware," he said, "for the completion of her cure it behoveth that thou go forth with all thy guards to the place where thou foundest her, nor shouldst thou forget the beast of black wood which was with her. Therein lies a devil and unless I exorcise him he will return to her and afflict her again."

So the King did as this physician asked. He visited the Princess and was filled with joy at the sweetness of her recovery and he bade his servants bathe her and dress her royally in fine robes and jewels. Then he and the Princess and all the army moved out to the field where first he had seen her and there on the sward* they had set up the ebony horse.

"My lord the King," said the Prince, "with thy leave and at thy word I will now proceed to fumigations and conjurations, that we may drive the evil spirit from this horse; but I must first place the damsel upon its back that we may observe whether or no there be a conjunction of spirits." And so, placing the Princess on the horse's back, he jumped into the saddle and urging her to cling to him tightly, he trilled the pin of ascent. The horse shuddered again as though it were drawing breath and forthwith rode up out of the field and over the heads of the King and his army and away across the seas to Persia.

Then was the marriage of the Princess to Prince Kamar al-Akmar indeed celebrated and messages of joy and consolation were despatched to the Princess's father that he might know of his daughter's happiness. As for the Persian magician, for all we know he continued to elaborate his spells in the Greek King's prison till the end of his days, and as for the ebony horse, the Emperor gained his wish and it was burned on a bonfire on the Prince's wedding-night.

* sward: grass

When this tale of the Ebony Horse was finished, the night was still dark over the Shah Shahryar's palace and so Dunyazad called upon her sister to tell them:-

THE STORY OF SINDBAD THE PORTER
AND SINDBAD THE SAILOR

In the days when Harun al-Rashid was Caliph in Baghdad there dwelt in that city a poor man who was known as Sindbad the Porter, for he made what living he could by carrying baggage on his head for hire.

One day, when the sun was at its hottest and his burden at its heaviest, he found himself beside the gate of a merchant's house. The courtyard beyond the gate was fresh with full-scented flowers, and from the rooms of the house there came the sounds of lutes and zithers and voices more beautiful than song-birds. "Truly, there is no God but Allah," said Sindbad the Porter, "and whom He wishes to raise He exalts and whom He wishes to abase He makes low," and, raising his voice he sang the verses:

> "Thou, Ruler of Heaven, hast placed the rich man
> There in his castle; the poor man at his gate.
> Thou, Ruler of Heaven, teach us Thy patience
> That we rejoice in Thee, whatever be our fate."

Now it so happened that the master of the house was walking in a room overlooking the street where Sindbad was singing, and he sent a servant to bring the porter before him. Thus it came about that he was led through rooms hung with fine tapestries and adorned with rich furnishings into the presence of the master: a man, grey with age but of resplendent nobility, sitting among a company of lords at tables garnished with meat and fruits and bowls of wine. Slave girls were playing instruments and singing and it seemed to the porter that he had entered Paradise.

"Welcome," said the master of the house; and he called for food and drink to be placed before his new guest, who, in wonderment, gave praise to Allah, washed his hands, and set to eating as though there might be no more tomorrows in his life. When he had finished, the master of the house welcomed him again and asked to know his name and calling.

"My name in Sindbad the Porter," said the man, "and I make my living by carrying other people's goods about the town for hire."

"Now that is passing strange," said the lord, "for my name too is Sindbad – although men call me Sindbad the Sailor – and I too have carried burdens on my back in my time. And when I heard you singing outside my house of the virtues of patience, it brought back to my mind the trials that I too have undergone, and it seemed to me a worthy act that I might offer you my hospitality and set before you the proof that suffering may lead to good cheer, and the way to prosperity may lie through hardship and privation."

And – as if she had been present at this banquet – Sheherezade began to tell Shah Shahryar of the Seven Voyages of Sindbad the Sailor just as he had told them to the Porter, his namesake.

The Tale of the Vanishing Island

I should have known from the start (he said) that my engaging to be a mariner was going to be a courtship with calamity. Indeed, if I had behaved myself, I need never have gone to sea at all, for I was born of a wealthy father and only reduced myself to the poverty of one like yourself, O Sindbad the Porter, by too much lavish eating and drinking and by giving myself unrestrained to the delights of youth. So it came about that I had to gather up what remnants of wealth I had and travel forth with them to trade in different quarters of the world from the Pillars of Hercules in the west to Serendib in the east.

We had not sailed long on my very first voyage before we came to an island that seemed like a little corner of Paradise. Trees and flowers blossomed on its fine soil and birds and small game were there for our eating. Accordingly we cast anchor and landed, and while some went to catch a fresh dinner for us, others set to lighting great fires for the cooking. Imagine our amazement, therefore, when the ship's master suddenly blew warnings to us on his clarion and summoned us back to the vessel. For this was no island at all that we had camped on, but a huge fish who had lain so long on the surface of the ocean that dust and sand had gathered on his back and nourished the undergrowth through which we hunted. Now the heat from our cooking-fires was so disturbing him that he grew uneasy. With a few quivers, like the first tremors of an earthquake, he flexed the muscles of his back and then suddenly he dived for the cool depths of the sea, leaving those of us who had not got back to the ship floating in an atoll of uprooted trees and bushes.

Only with the utmost difficulty did I escape from this wreckage of my fortune, and only by strange coincidence did I find again the goods and gear that I had left on board the ship; but I did not let this narrow encounter deter me from further voyaging, which led to:-

The Adventure of the Valley of Diamonds
I had taken ship, once more to go trading, and again we hove to at an island (but this time surely too large and mountainous to be a sleeping fish). While my fellows set about exploring and bringing aboard fresh water, I wandered off on my own to enjoy what I could find of the fruits of the island and to offer prayers and praises to the Omnipotent King.

Later I rested beneath a tree, where I fell asleep, and when I woke it was to find myself alone, for my companions had forgotten me and had sailed without me. Not knowing what to do, I set out to search the shore for help, but could find no trace of human habitation.

On climbing a tree, however, the better to see what lay inland, I observed, glinting in the sunshine, a huge white dome beyond the far side of a forest. So, with great difficulty, I made my way in that direction and eventually arrived at what seemed to be a strange building. It was smooth and pale as alabaster, with its walls curving up to meet the sky, but with no sign of doors or windows through which I might enter.

I set off to walk round it, and I had not gone fifty paces before the day darkened as though the sun had suddenly swept down below the horizon. As I peered westwards though, I saw that I had not been overtaken by a magic sunset, but that a gigantic bird was flying towards me, whose mighty body and widespread wings were hiding the sun from sight.

And in the darkness all suddenly became clear to me. For I remembered seamen's tales of a huge bird called a Rukh that was wont to lay eggs as big as a castle and that fed its young upon elephants. Surely this was just such an one, and surely the dome round which I was walking was none other than the Rukh's egg.

So it proved. The bird circled slowly out of the sun and came to rest on the surface of the dome, covering the shell with its breast and trailing its legs behind, towards the forest; and thus it fell asleep. As it slept though, I bethought me that this might prove an apt means for my escape, and I unwound my turban from my head, twisted it into a rope, and secured myself with it to one of the legs of the Rukh.

There I lay during the night, and in the morning the bird gave a great cry and rose from its nest on its mighty wings and flew with me over the ocean towards land. Eventually it came to rest on top of a high hill and here I speedily untied myself and watched as the bird took off again and swooped on some invisible object in the valley below. As it mounted towards heaven again though, I perceived that it held in its talons a monstrous wriggling serpent that it had plucked from the side of the hill, and as I followed the course that it had taken, I saw that I was lodged in a desert region of rocks and mountains, far less hospitable than the island from which I had flown.

Nevertheless, in search of water, I made my way towards the valley-bottom and discovered as I went that the whole place swarmed with snakes and serpents, each as big as a palm tree. It seemed that they spent much of the day hiding in holes and caves for fear of being attacked by the Rukhs, and all around their lairs, and spread across the valley floor, there glinted what looked like a pavement of glass. As I got nearer though, I saw that this was a delusion and that the ground was really scattered with diamonds, which lay as thick as the sands by the sea.

As I stood marvelling at all this wealth, lying amongst the serpents, I heard a strange bumping sound and I saw tumbling down the hill towards me a huge piece of meat, as it were the side of an ox; and as it fell, all sticky and bloody as it was, so it gathered to its surface the loose diamonds among which it was rolling. Then I remembered that I had heard tell of the stratagems of diamond-hunters, who proceeded in this way, tossing raw meat amongst the precious stones so that it might be lifted out of the valley by carnivorous birds from whom the diamonds could then be collected.

Trusting to this knowledge, I filled my pockets and my girdle and my turban with as many diamonds as I could and seized hold of the underside of the carcass, all raw and bloody as it was, and awaited events. Sure enough, before long, a great eagle swooped out of the sky and seized the meat in his talons and lifted it – and me – high out of the valley and brought us to ground by its nest on the other side of the mountain. In only a few moments, however, after our landing, there started a great racket of shouting and banging of gongs and from out of hiding came a group of diamond-hunters intent on holding the eagle at bay till they should pluck out whatever riches might be stuck to his dinner.

They were not a little amazed to find a man also entangled with the carcass, but when I told them my adventures and shared with them the stones that I had brought up from the valley, they wished that they might have such surprises every day. And so we returned to their camp and ate and drank until we all cried for Rukhs to come and carry us home.

As it happened though (said Sindbad to Sindbad), this was not the last of my encounters with the Rukh. For after several more years and several more voyages that bird became the direct cause of my adventure with:-

The Old Man of the Sea
I had set sail from Basra with a goodly company, and after several weeks voyaging we found ourselves once again on an island where the Rukhs had chosen to nest. I did not know this when we landed, nor had I ever told my shipmates of my own discovery of the egg, so when some of them saw the white dome rising above the tree-line they had no notion of the dangers that it might portend.

Several of them made their way to examine the objects and when (like me) they could find no sign on its smooth walls of what it might be, they began banging it with stones and beating it with fallen branches until suddenly, as all eggs will, it cracked open and they were like to be drowned in the watery fluid that streamed out over them.

As the flood subsided though, they perceived within the egg the body of the young Rukh and forthwith pulled it out and brought it back to the ship to be a handsome augmentation of our stores. But when I heard their story and recognized what they had done, I went straightway to the ship's master and urged him to set sail without delay. "Vengeance will be upon us otherwise," I said.

And I was right. For although the master called his men aboard and stood off from the island as fast as he could, it was not long before the sun was darkened by the wings of the returning birds. When they discovered the destruction wrought upon their egg, they began to utter piercing cries and rose vertically into the air to see who might have done such a thing. Nor did it take even their bird-brains long to determine that we were the culprits and we had barely got a league or two clear of the island before they appeared above us, each carrying in its claws a massive boulder brought from the tops of the mountains.

As soon as the he-Rukh came up with us, he let fall his rock from a great height. But the ship's master saw it coming and put the ship about so that the rock plunged into the sea – but with such violence that we were pitched high on the crest of the wave it made and looked down into the trough to see the bottom of the ocean laid momentarily bare. Then the she-Rukh let fall her boulder, which was bigger than that of her mate, and, as Destiny decreed, it fell straight on to the poop of our ship so that the vessel burst asunder in a thousand pieces and we were all cast into the sea.

Such was the tumult of the waves after this battering that there was no hope of us staying together, and before long I found myself separated from my companions and drifting aimlessly astride one of the planks of the broken ship. Through the intercession of Allah, however, I was eventually able to paddle my way towards the shore-line of an unknown coast and there I landed, yearning for food and water to refresh myself.

As I began to explore this new land, however, so it seemed to me that the Divine One had brought me to the edge of His Demesne. For here were fruits and flowers in abundance and clear streams, running with purest water, and all I had to do was to gather and drink my fill to be restored to life. So there I stayed till nightfall, hearing no voice and seeing no other man, and after giving thanks to the Most High and glorifying Him, I lay down and slept till morning.

Next day, following a stream in search of human habitations, I came upon a deep spring, flowing from a well, and there, beside the well, sat a venerable old man dressed in a skirt of palm fronds. I greeted him and he returned my salaam, but never a word he spoke. "Then tell me, nuncle," I said, "why do you sit silent here?" Again he bowed towards me and groaned, signalling with his hand as if to say that he wished to cross the channel from the well but could not do so. So I knelt down, that he might climb on my shoulders, and I stepped into the water and carried him to where he had pointed.

When he reached the other side, I stooped so that he might dismount, but as I did so he wound his legs more tightly round my neck and made no move to be gone. And when I looked at his legs and saw them black and rough like a buffalo's hide I took fright and sought to throw him from me, but to no avail. He clung to me and gripped my neck with his legs till I was nearly choked, and though I fell to the ground and writhed with the pain of it, still he stayed with me. Then he drummed his heels upon me and beat my back with his arms, which were like palm rods, and there was nothing I could do but rise and carry him where it seemed he wanted to go.

From that day forth he stayed as though pinioned upon my back. He drove me among the trees so that he might reach for the sweetest fruits, he lived and slept upon me as though I were there for his domestic comfort, and if ever I refused to do his bidding or loitered about too slowly he would bang me with his arms and feet, so that I was driven nearly mad.

"What reward is this for compassion?" I cried. "By Allah, if I live beyond this time I shall never more do any man service." And so in weariness I wandered on until one day we came to a place where there was an abundance of gourds fallen from their trees and drying in the sun. So I took a large dry gourd, cut it open, and hollowed it out and cleaned it. Then I gathered grapes which grew on a vine nearby and squeezed them into the gourd till it was full of their juice, and I stopped up its mouth and left it in the sun that it might ferment and become strong wine. In this way I brewed a potion to sustain me through my troubles and bring me some measure of cheerfulness.

One day, as I was unstoppering one of my gourds of wine, the Old Man on my back signed to me that he wished to know what I was drinking. "Ha ha!" I cried, "it is such liquor as makes even porters happy," and I began to dance and reel among the trees with the old man jogging on my shoulders. When he realized how frolicsome the wine appeared to make me, he began drumming on my head and gurgling as much as to say that he, too, wanted a portion. So I passed up a gourd full of the fermented brew and he drained it to the dregs and hurled it into the forest and at once began jigging up and down, mouthing strange noises, which I took to be his kind of singing:

"yorhorlorlorlor,
yorhorlorlorlor,
yorhorlorlorlorkus
yorhorlorlorlor!"

And as the fumes of the wine rolled round his brain so his side-muscles and his limbs relaxed and I was at last able to tip him off my shoulders on to the ground – yorhorlorlorlor!

There he lay, out of his senses with drunkenness. So I went among the trees and found a great stone and smote him on the head with it, that he might never more be a curse to travellers. Then I took my way back to the sea-coast and dwelt in peace, tending my sores, until I saw the sail of a passing ship and was able to signal to it to put in and rescue me.

When the sailors questioned me as to who I was and how I came to be stranded on this coast, they marvelled to hear of my adventure with the creature that tormented me. "For you should know," they said, "that he is spoken of in these parts as Sheikh-a-Bahr, which is to say the Old Man of the Sea, and none but you has ever borne that burden and survived. For those that he traps he marches till they die under him, and then he eats them … "

So (said Sindbad the Sailor to Sindbad the Porter),

thus may you see how I have done my share of carrying in the world, but such has been my patience under oppression and my perseverance through so many voyages that I came to safe harbour here at last – and since the days are long gone since I swore never to show compassion, and since thou art well-met as a man of my name, let us render praise to Allah that we live in a world so full of His mercies that we shall all at last come safe to shore.

And Sindbad the Sailor and Sindbad the Porter drank and made merry and were as brothers from that day forth.

When she had concluded the story of the strange adventures of Sindbad the Sailor, Sheherezade perceived that the dawn was still below the horizon and she told the Shah Shahryar of an unusual event. Some time before, it seems, passing incognito through the market-place on her way to the hammam baths, she had encountered a crowd of people listening to stories from a traveller, recently arrived. He was a stranger from the north, speaking a rustic dialect, but he told stories that he said were famed in his territory; and Sheherezade had attended to the tales that he told. "Now my Lord," she said to the Shah Shahryar, "from my recollections of this man, let me seek to copy something of his strange speech and recount to you the stories that he told." And as the nights passed, Sheherezade told the Shah:-

THE STORY OF ALI BABA AND THE FORTY THIEVES

The Cave

One time, many years back, there were two brothers: one a jolly man, round as a sweet apple, who was called Ali Baba; the other thin, and mean as a creaking door, and he was called Kasim. Kasim had married a woman as stingy as himself – the daughter of a merchant down in the market – and when that one took his trade to Heaven, Mr and Mrs Kasim continued in his place and they just got meaner and meaner, and richer and richer.

As for Ali Baba though, he had married a feckless, prodigal lady and they never had a penny to their names. Every day Ali Baba would take three asses into the nearby forest, where he would load them up with brushwood and dry timber to sell round the streets, but whatever he earned he and Mrs Ali Baba would spend, living the good life.

Well, one day he was sitting in the forest, munching a pitta bread sandwich for his dinner, when he heard a jingling of bridles and felt the ground beneath him quiver with the tread of horses' hoofs: many horses, many hoofs. So being a prudent chap – especially when pitta bread sandwiches were on the go – and thinking that this might be a notorious band of forest outlaws, he pushed his asses deep into the undergrowth and shinned up a nearby tree, to be well out of sight when they came along.

And just as well that he did. For this was indeed a bunch of robbers – forty men with horses and baggage and who knows what – and as they got to the tree where Ali Baba was hiding they stopped and their chief went up to a wall of rock that rose out of the forest floor opposite the tree. The chief looked at the wall of rock. The wall of rock looked at the chief. Then the chief said, "Open, Sesame!" – and straightway, with a noise like a thousand grindstones, part of the rock slid aside to make a great doorway, and the chief and his men rode inside with their baggage. Then the rock slid closed behind them.

"Allah protect us all," said Ali Baba up in his tree; and he stayed there, not daring to finish his dinner and hoping that his asses wouldn't start braying, for fear he'd be discovered and done away with on the spot. Eventually the rock-door slid open again and the chief, their captain, rode out, stopping on the threshold to count the men who followed him – one to thirty-nine. When he was sure they were all there he turned to the rock and said, "Shut, Sesame!" and the door slid to and the robbers trotted away.

When he was sure they were all gone, Ali Baba came down from the tree, reckoning to get home as fast as he could. But when he saw the rock-wall, standing there so inviting-like, he couldn't stop himself from saying, "Open, Sesame!" and – squeak, grind, rumble – the door opened for him too.

Well, that could clearly be taken as a sign – from Earth, if not from Heaven – so Ali Baba stepped into the cleft to see what he could see. Sheesh! High up in the ceiling of the rock there had been fashioned cunning air-holes and bullseye windows*, and by the light that streamed down Ali Baba could see great bales of embroidered cloths, camel-loads of silks and brocades, mounds of carpets, and bags and sacks full of gold and jewels. Surely not just this band of robbers, but their fathers and grandfathers must have been hiding their loot in this cave for more years than they had donkeys.

Although the rock-door had rumbled shut behind him when he'd got inside the cavern, Ali Baba kept calm, and after he'd looked at all the heaps of treasure he turned and said, "Open, Sesame!" and the door obediently rumbled open. Thereupon he went and found his three asses, brought them to the cave and loaded them with sacks of gold, hidden by a covering of brushwood and kindling. Then he said, "Shut, Sesame!" and made off back home as fast as his poor tottering animals would let him.

The Kitchen Scales
When Ali Baba got to the yard by his house he drove in the asses and carefully shut the gate so no one would see what he was up to. Then he began to unload the covering of brushwood so that he could get at the gold. But Mrs Ali Baba, hearing the coins clink and feeling the heavy, knobbly leather bags, straightway thought her man had been up to no good and went to fetch her rolling-pin so that she could talk to him about living an honest life.

Before she could get into the swing of her lecture though, Ali Baba explained what had happened and

---

* bullseye windows: small round windows of thick glass

poured out on the kitchen table some of the golden dinars and sovereigns and asrafis that he had collected from the cave. This caused her to have second thoughts about questions of honesty, and, being of an orderly disposition, she began to count up the coins and stack them according to their values.

"You daft duck," said Ali Baba, "you'll never get through with that all night, and we'll have money piled up to the ceiling. Why don't we just dig a nice hole in the floor and tip it all in; then we can call on it whenever we want a treat."

"Well, you're right," said his wife, "but even so it would be nice to know roughly what we've got. Why don't we weigh it? I'll go round and borrow Mrs Kasim's scales and I'll weigh the stuff while you're digging the hole."

So Mrs Ali Baba went round to her sister-in-law's and asked to borrow her kitchen scales. "Funny," thought Mrs Kasim, "funny. She's never been that wild about cooking before; what's she after with these scales?" and while she pretended to hunt them out from the bottom of a cupboard she secretly smeared some honey over the pan of the balance. "That should tell us something," she said to herself.

Well, the Ali Babas got on with their weighing and their digging, and when they'd finished they carefully stowed all their winnings away under the kitchen floor and Mrs Ali Baba took the scales back to Mrs Kasim – and of course she hadn't bothered to wash them up or anything before she left. So when Mrs Kasim came to inspect them, once Ali Baba's wife had gone home, what should she see stuck to the golden honey but a golden coin. "Asrafis!" she yelled, "asrafis! Those good-for-nothing Ali Babas – they've not just laid hold of some cash somewhere, but they're having to weigh out asrafis on my scales as though they were corn husks!" And when old squinty Kasim came back from his shop, she told him what had happened and packed him off round to his brother's to find out what was the beginning and the end of it all.

"What's this, then?" said Kasim to Ali Baba. "Just look at you. Holes in your best tunic – and yet you have to borrow my wife's scales to weigh out your gold. What's going on?"

"Don't know what you're talking about," said Ali Baba.

"Look at this then," said Kasim; and he held up the asrafi, still sticky with honey. "Now, what's going on?"

Well, Ali Baba had known his brother and his brother's wife long enough to judge when he could make monkeys out of them and when he couldn't, and this time he saw was a time for plain-dealing. He told Kasim about his adventure in the forest and his discovery of the robbers' gold and how he'd brought back a bag or two to take care of. But that wasn't enough for Kasim.

"If you don't tell me exactly where that place is, and exactly what I have to do to get in, then I'll take you round to the magistrate tomorrow and you can explain to him how you came by so much gold."

Kasim's Come-uppance
There was nothing to be done about it. Ali Baba had to tell his brother the exact whereabouts of the cave in the forest, and the exact password for getting into it; and the next day Kasim hired a dozen mules and

set off to see what he could see. Everything fitted: track through the forest; clearing; wall of rock; and the magic words. "Open, Sesame!" said Kasim, and the door rolled backwards and in he went with his bags and satchels to collect up whatever winnings he could find.

As was usual, the rock-door had rumbled shut behind Kasim when he'd gone in; but after he'd stuffed all his baggage full of gold and jewels and suchlike he couldn't for the life of him remember how to get it open again. "Open, Barley!" he said – recollecting that the magic had to do with some sort of seed – "Open, Millet! Open, Poppy-head!" (and even, in a reckless effort to be funny, "Open, Cumin!"). But it was all to no avail. The door stayed shut, nor did he have any hope of climbing the smooth walls of the cave up to its high windows. The gold in his sacks glinted at him like grinning teeth.

Then he heard a commotion outside. For the robber band, riding past their hide-out, were surprised to see a great team of mules browsing around outside the door – for Kasim had foolishly not bothered to tether them in the under-brush the way Ali Baba had done. The captain rode up to the door and Kasim, wild with anguish, heard him yell the magic words, "Open, Sesame!" and the rock began to trundle sideways. What could he do? Hoping to gain something from surprise he rushed out of the cave as soon as there was a gap wide enough for him to do so, but, alas! he ran full tilt into the captain, and before the door had finished its opening the robbers had thrown him to the ground and chopped him in half.

They were dumbfounded. How could this stranger

have found his way into their lair? How had he known of their riches, that he'd brought all these sacks to carry them away? Who else might be in the know?

Well, one thing was for sure. If this burglar had got any accomplices then they'd better look out. So the captain ordered his men to divide up the two bits of Kasim's dead body and they hung two quarters of Kasim outside the door and two quarters inside as a warning to those who would be warned.

Coping with the Corpse

Back at home, Mrs Kasim was getting more and more worried. By the time it got dark and her man not back yet, she went round to Ali Baba's to see what might be done. "Twelve mules," she said, "and all those sacks; we must be able to find him somewhere." And Ali Baba tried to comfort her and promised that he'd start off on a search as soon as it was light.

This he did. He took some of his own asses and made off like he was collecting firewood as usual, and he headed for the robbers' cave. As soon as he got there and saw the bloody bits of Kasim hanging outside the door he settled that his brother wasn't such a bright chap after all and – taking a chance that no one was inside – he called to the door to open.

Well, when he saw the other bits of Kasim, and Kasim's sacks still full of gold in there, he realized what had happened. He straightway bundled as much as he could of his brother and his brother's treasure into his own sacks, covered everything with brushwood, and set off home. He didn't fancy giving the lads a second chance with their cleavers.

70

When he got home he handed over the sacks of gold to his wife to take care of, and then he took the asses round to Kasim's house to break the bad news to Mrs Kasim. Knock, knock: he tapped at the door. But the door was opened not by Mrs Kasim but by Morgiana, her body slave, who was a pretty bright lass, and as soon as she'd let him in to the courtyard, Ali Baba told her the whole dreadful story.

"Brother of my lady's lord," said Morgiana, "this is thorny brushwood you are tangling with. I have some knowledge of that captain and his men, and when they find out that someone has called in to collect Kasim and all his gold they won't rest till they have found him. We must act with the greatest circumspection."

By this time Mrs Kasim had also appeared in the courtyard, and when they broke the news to her about the dismemberment of her poor husband, they were hard put to it to stop her going at once into the street and setting up an instant wake. But Ali Baba promised that he would marry her himself, once the time of her mourning was over (for such is the custom of that place), and together they listened to the plan that Morgiana had devised.

This is how it happened. When morning came, Morgiana went down to the druggist's stall in the bazaar, seeking powerful medicine for a dangerous sickness. "Who is so ill that he needs this?" asked the druggist; and Morgiana told him it was her master. The next day she went there again and asked him for a repeat prescription, and the druggist shook his head sagely, as much as to say that no help could be expected when things were as bad as that.

That, of course, was exactly what Morgiana had

71

intended, and it therefore came as no surprise to Kasim's neighbours and to all the merchants in the bazaar when, next day, Morgiana declared that her master was dead and that his wife and his brother and the wife of his brother were prostrate with grief. To her had fallen the business of preparing the funeral.

Well, those preparations were not exactly conventional. That night Morgiana betook herself to the shop of one Baba Mustafa, a tailor and maker of shrouds and grave-cloths, a man well-advanced in years. Knocking at his door she proffered him a gold piece and asked him if he would accompany her on a secret journey. This he was not inclined to do and it took another asrafi before he allowed her to blindfold his eyes and lead him through streets and byways into the house and into the darkened room where the remains of Kasim were lying.

"Well, master tailor," said Morgiana, "out with your needle and sew me up this body as good as new; then when you've done, take this cloth and make me a shroud for him, for he must be buried tomorrow." So Baba Mustafa set to with his needle and by the time that all was finished he was glad enough to accept a purseful of asrafis and to allow himself once more to be blindfolded and led back through the streets and alley-ways to his tailor's shop.

*Calcification**
Meanwhile, there was consternation among the forty thieves. For when they returned to their cave after a day of the usual villainies they found not

* calcification: chalkiness

only that Kasim-outside-the-door, but also Kasim-inside-the-door, had disappeared – and all his sacks of booty too. The secret of the Open Sesame was known, but how could they discover the knower?

"A plan, captain," said one of the gang, and went on to explain how he might dress up like a foreign merchant and go into the town seeking information about who had died recently and who had fallen upon easy times. That way they might be able to work out who their sneaky visitor had been.

"Very well," said the captain; so the fellow burrowed about among their bags of garments and turbans and sashes until he had got himself up to look like some wealthy trader from out of town. Then he set off for the bazaar, getting there first thing in the morning so that he could see as many of the merchants as possible.

Not much was doing when he arrived – most of the shops were still shut up – but there, sitting in the dawn light was Baba Mustafa, sewing away to catch up with the time he'd lost while he'd been attending to Kasim. "Well," said the robber, "what are you up to then? How can you see to sew stitches before it's properly light?"

"Oho," said Baba Mustafa, "it's plain you're not from these parts, I've been known for my sharp eyes longer than you've been born. Whyd'y'know, someone even came along the other day to get me to sew up the bits of a dead body in a room without any light at all. And I made the chap's shroud too."

"You're joking," said the robber. "You're a tailor, not a surgeon. How could you do a thing like that?"

"Never you mind," said Baba Mustafa, "it's nowt to do with you."

"Well I do mind," said the robber, clinking a couple of gold pieces in the palm of his hand, "I'd just like to see that place where you did a thing like that."

"Well, that's not easy," said the tailor, "because I never saw it. Whoever wanted the job done put a blindfold on me and took me through the streets as if I were a nervy horse."

"Hmm," said the robber, and he put down his asrafis by the tailor's stool.

"Now what about this. If I were to blindfold you too, and start you off from here, why shouldn't someone with your sharp eyes have a sharp memory too, and why shouldn't you be able to remember how the journey went?"

And that's just what occurred. The robber put one of his sashes round the tailor's eyes and the tailor slowly retraced the steps that he'd made when Morgiana led him; round corners, down alley-ways, right to the front door of Kasim's house. "That's the one," he said, "that's where they live – and very generous they were too – good pay I got for traipsing round here and doing all that work." Which hint was taken by the robber, who gave Baba Mustafa a little bag of dinars and wished him good tailoring for the rest of his days. Then, when Mustafa had left the street, the robber pulled a piece of chalk out of his wallet, chalked a big white cross on Kasim's door and went back to report to his chief down in the forest.

A few minutes later, out comes Morgiana to do the day's shopping. She couldn't help noticing that someone had lately put a big white cross on the front door, and, having a suspicious turn of mind, it struck her that that someone might be up to no good. So she went back indoors and found a piece of white chalk and she went round the street putting crosses on everyone's doors.

Thus it came about that when the robber came back to the town with the captain, all ready to show him the house, he found a streetful of chalk-marks and couldn't for the life of him decide which was his and which was not. So the captain, in a fine fury, hauled him off back to the forest and had his head chopped off for being a pestiferous nuisance, and thereupon sent Robber Number Two to see if he could do any better.

Well the same thing happened to Robber Number Two as to Robber Number One. He found Baba Mustafa, jingled gold pieces at him, got shown the house, and this time, with a touch of genius, he made a red cross immediately next to the original white one. Then he went back to the forest – and Baba Mustafa went back to his shop with a growing belief that golden asrafis were being shovelled up like desert sand.

Unfortunately for Robber Number Two the same sequence of events didn't leave off there. For once again Morgiana spotted the mark on the door and once again she found some chalk to match, so that when the man proudly brought his chief down the street, he was dismayed to see that red crosses now adorned all the doorways, along with the white ones. The house remained inscrutable and there was nothing for it except a return to the forest and off with his head as well.

The Captain's Craft
By this time the captain was starting to have doubts about the intelligence of his troops, so he decided

that he would go and find the house for himself (at least he couldn't chop his own head off if he missed it). Thus more tours of the streets were made; more gold pieces slid into the hands of Baba Mustafa; but the captain took no pains to mark the door but rather marked inside his head the whole placing and appearance of the house so that he would recognize it again. Then he went back to his men and propounded the following plot:

"Comrades: I have no doubt that I have found the house where is lodged the source of all our trouble and I'm going to propose an assault that will settle accounts for good. All forty of us – uh – no – sorry – um – all thirty-eight of us will travel to the town this evening. I shall travel as a sheikh dealing in oil and I shall take with me twenty – er – nineteen mules, each with two jars yoked across its back. One of these jars will indeed be filled with oil, but the other thirty-seven will contain your good selves, comfortably stowed, and armed with scimitars, cutlasses, daggers or whatever weapons best take your fancy. We will gain admission to the house and in the dark hours of night I shall release you from your jars and we shall rise up and slay the whole household."

So it was. The oil-sheikh and his mule rode down to the city and by tortuous* journeyings made their way to Kasim's house where Ali Baba and Mrs Ali Baba were now living. (They were enjoying themselves as never before, being looked after by Morgiana and Kasim's other servants and helping Mrs Kasim to get accustomed to her grief and to the prospect of becoming another wife for Ali Baba.)

* tortuous: roundabout, twisted

As the captain and his entourage* came up to the house Ali Baba himself was there, strolling to and fro enjoying the evening air after his supper. The captain salaamed. "My lord," he said, "many and many a time I have come to this town selling my oil, but never before have I arrived so late. I am perplexed as to where I might rest for the night, unburden my mules and give them their fodder. Is it possible that we could tarry here in your courtyard?"

Well, Ali Baba was by nature an hospitable man and liked nothing better than company, so he welcomed the oil-sheikh to his courtyard and gave orders to Morgiana to prepare supper and a guest room for the traveller. (Nor did Ali Baba in any way recognize the sheikh for who he was. The disguise was perfect, and, in any case, he had only seen and heard the captain before when he'd been perched up in that tree with his teeth rattling and his ears humming.)

The captain made much ado of feeding his mules and unloading his jars. As he did so, he whispered to each of his men that he was to wait for a summons in the middle of the night, when they should all rise from out their jars and slaughter the household. Then the captain went indoors to enjoy his supper.

The Kitchener's Craft
Now it so happened that, half-way through the evening, while Morgiana was doing the dishes, the lamps began to flicker and fail (it's a well-known characteristic of lamps that when one goes they all go). When Morgiana went to her cruse* to replenish

* entourage: company
* cruse: earthenware pot

the supply she was dismayed to discover that the cruse was empty. A black night threatened.

"What's the worry?" said Abdullah, one of the skivvy-boys, "there's thirty-eight jars of the stuff out there in the courtyard; I'm sure our friend won't miss a ladle or two off the top of one of them." So Morgiana picked up the cruse and went out to where the thirty-eight jars were lined up and began to see if she could find one that would open. Well – you can guess she was a bit startled when, first jar that she came to, she heard a voice whispering out at her, "Is it time now?" (for the chap in the jar thought she was the captain coming to start things moving). But Morgiana came to her senses pretty quick, realized that this was not a customary thing for oil-jars to say, and replied huskily, "No; the time is not yet." And so it went on. Jar by jar she walked down the courtyard, each time hearing, "Is it time now?" and each time replying, "No; the time is not yet," till she got to the last jar of all, where she found what she'd first come to seek.

"May Allah protect us, the Compassionating, the Compassionate," she said to herself as she filled the cruse. "My lord has given lodging to this sheikh and it seems that this sheikh is going to pay him out with a mule train of bandits"; and when she got back to the kitchen she trimmed her lamps and set a great cauldron to heat on the fire. Then she took Abdullah with her out to the yard, and between them they manhandled the one full jar of oil into the kitchen and tipped it all into the cauldron.

By dint of much stirring and stoking the oil soon

began to seethe and bubble in the cauldron. Morgiana then ladled some of its contents into a can, went out to the courtyard and tipped the contents into the first jar, scalding the fellow in it to death. And so, can by can and jar by jar, she went down the line of thirty-seven thieves, making an end of each and every one of them.

Not long after this, the captain roused himself up, opened his window, and cracked his whip out over the courtyard as a signal that the assault should begin. Nothing happened. He cracked the whip again. Still nothing.

So cursing his men for falling asleep, but fearing to make too much row, he crept out to the yard to take matters into his own hands. When he got out there, though, he was startled by the smell of oil and seething flesh, and when he touched the first jar he found it reeking hot and he realized that his plot was discovered and that of all the forty thieves he was now the last one left. There was nothing for it but to make his escape as quick as he could, so he climbed over the garden wall and made the best of his way back to his cave to think up some new stratagem for revenge.

Next morning, when Ali Baba passed through the courtyard, he was surprised to see the mules still stabled and the jars still waiting to be taken to the market. He sent for Morgiana and asked her to rouse the sheikh who must surely have overslept. "No oil-sheikh he," said Morgiana, "but a bandit-chief, and it's his men who are sleeping." And she took Ali Baba down the line of jars, showing him their contents and telling him all that had happened. They settled between them that, what with the crosses on the doors and the trick with the oil, they were up against the gang of the forty thieves, but what had happened to the captain and the other two was more than they could tell.

"We may have done for them at the moment," said Morgiana, "but I don't reckon that's the last we'll see of that captain." With that, she and Ali Baba went down to the tool shed, picked out a couple of shovels, and dug a large pit where they quietly buried their intruders.

How It Ended

Once again Morgiana was right, of course. The captain sat in his cave for a few days, brooding on his bad luck, then he gathered up some of his stock of silks and embroidered cloths and took himself off to the town in the guise of a merchant. He rented a pitch in the bazaar and started trading.

Well, as the days and weeks went by he put himself out to be friendly to all his fellow merchants – not least to one Khwajah Hassan, who was the son of our late friend Kasim and who was carrying on with his father's business. The captain took much pains to cultivate this young man, giving him presents and standing him hot suppers, while for his part Khwajah Hassan was flattered to be taken up by a man who seemed to know so much of the ways of the world.

Now, one day Khwajah Hassan had the idea that he would surprise the captain with a return treat. He fixed with Morgiana that she would be ready to prepare a fancy dinner for his new friend and then – when the day's trading was over – he suggested to the captain that they might take a little stroll together. "Let me show you some pretty bits of the Garden District," he said, and he took the captain down those streets and alley-ways that the captain had traversed so recently with Baba Mustafa the tailor. "What am I to do about this?" thought he to himself – and privily* fingered the dagger that he always kept tucked in his sash.

When they reached Kasim's old house, where Ali Baba was still living comfortably with Mrs Ali Baba, Mrs Kasim, and all Kasim's former servants, Khwajah Hassan stopped. "Well, now," he said, "just see where we've got to. This is my uncle's house; why don't we knock on the door and see if he's in?" The captain, still puzzled by what was going on, didn't know what to say about that, and while he was still um-ing and er-ing Morgiana opened the door and (as she'd fixed with Khwajah Hassan) straightway asked them both in to supper.

This seemed to the captain an opportunity for revenge that had been sent direct from Allah, but he set about a canny reply. "I am beholden to the house," he said with great formality, "and to the master of the house for the honour of such hospitality, but alas, I cannot accept; allow me to depart and tarry no longer."

As he'd expected, they wouldn't hear of it, and indeed, Ali Baba himself came to the door to help prevail upon his nephew's new-found friend to give way. "Why," said Ali Baba, "we have heard such reports of your kindness and your wisdom that we would fain entertain you this evening and hear more

* privily: secretly

81

of your adventures walking up and down in the world."

"Alas again," said the captain, "I long to accept your gracious invitation, but you must know that I have for many years suffered an ailment of the belly and I am now ordered by my physician never to eat food with salt in it."

"What matter? What matter?" said Ali Baba, "the meats are not yet cooked. We will prepare dinner without any salt," and he hauled the captain into the best sitting-room and ordered Morgiana to tell the cook "no salt".

"No salt?" thought Morgiana, "no salt … funny … now what kind of ailment puts a bar on salt?" and before she left for the kitchen, she looked keenly at Khwajah Hassan's guest and she understood everything. For here surely, under his smooth disguise, was the one-time oil-sheikh, one-time leader of the forty thieves, and by not taking salt with his host he would be under no obligation of custom or of the law of the Prophet, to restrain whatever violent intentions he might harbour. "So-ho!" she thought, "this fellow is up to no good and must be attended to."

As the conversation and the salt-less dinner proceeded therefore, Morgiana took care to observe the company closely, and was not surprised to see the guest of honour fussing and fiddling from time to time with his sash, where, eventually, she perceived what could only be the handle of a hidden poniard*. (And, for his part, as he fussed and fiddled, the captain thought, "How long, how long must I still

* poniard: small dagger

82

endure this boring gossip? How soon can we get rid of this tiresome servant girl and her attendants, so I can get down to the point of the evening?")

Morgiana however, besought Ali Baba that, while they enjoyed the last of their dinner, she might dance for them, the better to show zeal for their guest's entertainment and – to the captain's great impatience – Ali Baba agreed. So Morgiana left the supper-room and went to her closet where she found a great store of muslins, such as dancers wear. She dressed herself in a transparent veiling, bound a fine turban round her head, and placed within the sash at her waist a dagger rich in filigree and jewellery. Then she found the boy Abdullah, gave him a tambourine, and ordered him to accompany her in her dance.

Thus, with Abdullah rattling the tambourine, Morgiana entered the supper-room, bowed low to the assembled company, and began to cavort round the middle of the floor. She flung veils around, rather like the historic Salome, all the time watching the glinting eyes of the captain of the forty thieves and she saw a flicker of understanding, and as his hand moved towards his sash, she pulled out her own dagger and lunged at him, thrusting it into his heart.

Uproar! "The girl's gone mad!" cried Ali Baba. "What a way to treat a guest!" cried Khwajah Hassan. "Rattle, rattle," went the tambourine. But Morgiana drew back and bowed to everyone. "Not mad, my lord," she said to Ali Baba, "but prudent in my master's service," and she showed him the dagger hidden in the captain's sash and explained the sure purpose of his refusing to eat salt.

Then Ali Baba did indeed recognize him as the

man he had first seen so long ago, down in the forest, crying "Open Sesame!"; the man who had sought his hospitality as oil-sheikh and brought into his courtyard a mule train of thieves. And he blessed Morgiana for her wit and straightway married her to his nephew Khwajah Hassan who, being a son of Kasim, was hardly a match for her beauty or her intelligence. He also gathered together his old train of asses and returned to the robbers' cave to clear it of all its treasure. Then he, and Mrs Ali Baba, and she who had once been Mrs Kasim, and all the rest of them lived (as the saying goes) happily ever after.

And when Sheherezade had told the story of Ali Baba, which she had got from the stranger from the north, she went on to tell another which she had heard from him:-

THE STORY OF ALADDIN AND THE SLAVE OF THE LAMP

The Uncle
Times past, way off in China, in the city of all cities, there was a good-for-nothing fellow called Aladdin. His dad was a tailor, of the Tuanki family, and the idea was that Aladdin would be a tailor too, but he didn't set much store by that for a game of marbles. So instead of learning his trade he hung around street corners with a lot of tykes no better than himself. If they had any money they gambled it away; if they didn't have any they were up to no good till they got some.

Having a son who racketed around like that was bad news for the tailor. He tried all ways to get the boy to shape up, but it was no good, and in the end the chap worried himself into an early grave. There was nothing for it, then, but Aladdin's mum had to sell up the shop, and the best she could do to keep the two of them out of the workhouse was to take up spinning. Not a profitable trade. She had to spin from sun-up to midnight just to pay the rent.

Now it so happened that half-way round the world, in Africa, there lived at this time a Moorish magician. He was a chap who'd spent a lot of time perfecting the arts of geomancy (which is a bit like telling fortunes from tea-leaves, but you do it with sand).

Anyway, with his sand and his sand-table he'd discovered that there was a fortune to be found over in China, but that he'd probably need the help of a down-and-out ne'er-do-well called Aladdin to do some of the dirty work.

So the Moorish magician set off for China; and when he got to the city of all cities he set about making a tour of all the back streets till he should come across the Aladdin he was looking for. Well, that wasn't so hard. By this time young Aladdin's reputation as a tear-away was pretty widely known and the magician wasn't long in discovering him with his mates – tying oil-pots to a stray dog's tail, or some such monkey business.

The Moorish magician stood there watching for a bit; then he goes up to the boy, flings his arms round him, hugs him, kisses him and I don't know what-all, and says, "Aladdin! Oh, Aladdin! son of my dear old brother; say hello to your long-lost uncle!"

Well – far from saying hello, Aladdin wasn't up to saying anything at all. Nobody'd ever told him that he'd got an uncle, long-lost or otherwise, and he hadn't a clue what to do next. But the uncle had. After a lot more fussing he opened up his purse and took out a handful of golden dinars. "Oh my dear nephew," says he, "take these – take these as a token of all the years that have passed us by – you and me and your dear mother and father (may Allah rest his soul). Go home to your mother and give her my greetings; tell her I'm back from all my wanderings and that tomorrow night, God willing, we'll get together to talk about old times. Here – " (pulling more dinars out of his purse), "make sure you lay on a nice supper; and now just tell me how I get round to your house and we'll meet again tomorrow."

So Aladdin told him where he lived and then rushed off there to give the news to his mum. She was pretty surprised to see him, because he didn't usually come home that early, and she was still more surprised when he told her about his uncle. "What uncle?" she said. "First I've heard of any uncles," and she reckoned it was some fancy excuse to explain how he'd come by all that gold. But Aladdin stuck to his story and made so much to-do about fixing a proper supper the next night that she didn't see she'd much alternative. So she did as he suggested, laid in more steaks and jam-puddings and jars of wine than she'd seen in the last twenty years, and sat back to see what would happen.

Sure enough, next evening, there's a ring at the bell and there stands the magician. "Good evening, Mrs Tuanki," says he, "I know this is a surprise, and I know it's short notice and all that, but now I'm back, I've just got to make amends for being such a hopeless brother-in-law to you ... " And so he went on; and the end of it all was that she swallowed the lot (including the nice supper), and from that day on Aladdin had an uncle and the Tuanki family had three good meals a day.

The Cave

The magician worked fast to get Aladdin into a biddable frame of mind. Along with paying the back-rent and suchlike, he said he'd make some inquiries about having the boy apprenticed to the brokers down in the market – and what with promising to set him up in business and buy him

87

some smart clothes, he soon had him trotting around like a tame poodle. They'd go into town, look at all the monuments, eat dinner, and even wander round the public bits of the Sultan's palace, while Aladdin's uncle explained to him all the hierarchies and customs of the state.

So Aladdin wasn't surprised when one day his uncle turned up and suggested a walk in the other direction. "If you'd like to come with me into the country," he said, "I'll show you a sight beside which everything we've seen together so far will be nothing" – a remark pretty well guaranteed to encourage even a slouch like Aladdin to buckle on his shoes.

Off they went. First of all through gardens at the side of the town, each with its own pretty little pavilion or pagoda, then into open country, and then into a rocky valley that led up to the hills. "What's all this about?" said Aladdin, who'd never set foot out of the city gate before this. "Why do we want to be traipsing about in this rough country when we might be having a picnic or something back in those gardens?"

"Never you mind," said his uncle, "you keep by me and you'll see gardens beyond anything the Kings of the World can manage." And he kept walking into the rocky valley.

Eventually they got to a little flat part covered with small boulders.

"Right," said the magician, "now you hunt around here and find me some sticks and stuff to make a fire" – which was a pretty tall order since most of the valley bottom was all stones. But Aladdin was really keyed-up to know what this uncle of his was up to, so he worked away more than he'd ever done before at finding whatever bits of chippings and brushwood he could. As he brought them along, the magician made him pile them up in a little circle that he'd marked among the boulders, and while Aladdin was fossicking around, he secretly poured on some powder that he'd hidden in a flask underneath his robe.

When they'd got a fair pile of tinder together the magician walked round it with his staff, conjuring smoke and fire out of the brushwood, and as the fire took hold he began to mutter cabbalistic* words over it. Then, suddenly – whump! – the whole lot exploded with a force that shook the floor of the valley. Aladdin was scared out of his wits and was all for heading back to town as fast as possible, but his uncle caught him a clip round the head that just about knocked his back teeth out and caused him to tumble to the ground.

"Hey – what's that in aid of?" he said, suddenly overcome with serious doubts about how good the intentions of his new relation really were. "All right – all right – easy does it, my dear nephew," said the magician, who didn't want Aladdin running off after all the trouble he'd had to get him there.

"Cruel-to-be-kind, you know. If I'm to show you all these marvels then I can't have you clearing off home before we've even started. Now look there where the fire was." And Aladdin looked – and what he saw among the ashes was a big marble slab with a large copper ring sticking out of the middle of it.

* cabbalistic: secret

"Treasure," said the magician; "treasure, buried in your name, such that you are the only one who can redeem it. Do now as I say and you'll become richer than all the Sultans of the East," and he directed Aladdin to pull up the marble slab.

Aladdin took hold of the copper ring and heaved, but the slab wouldn't budge. He heaved again till he almost bust a gut, and the slab still wouldn't budge. "Oh, Aladdin, Aladdin, son of my brother, what did I say," said the magician, "the treasure may be yours to redeem, but you can't just heave away at that slab like a navvy. Pull the ring, and as you pull, recite your name, and your father's name and your mother's name and the stone will come up."

So Aladdin pulled again, saying these names like a prayer, and lo and behold! up came the slab as though it was on oiled bearings, and there below was a dark cave with steps going down. "Bravo!" said the magician, "well done! Now here is what you must manage next:

You must enter that cavern and go down the twelve steps before you;
at the bottom you will find a passage-way of four secret chambers,
and in each chamber you will find four marble tables,
and on each table you will find four golden jars,
and in each jar you will find gold and gems and jewels;

but don't put your hands on any of it and don't let your body or your garments or the hem of your robe touch any of it, otherwise you will be turned into a *black stone*. Instead, go carefully through each of the chambers and when you get to the end of the fourth one you will see in front of you a plain door with a copper handle. Take hold of that handle and repeat again the names of power and you will be able to open the door.

"The other side of the door," said the magician, "is a garden, whose like is not to be found this side of Paradise. It is laid out with lawns and pathways, streams and fountains, fruit trees and flowers, of a kind beyond description – but do not be waylaid. You must take a path from the door that winds for fifty cubits* until it comes to an open pavilion, and in that pavilion you will see a ladder of thirty rungs, and at the top of that ladder you will see a Lamp suspended from the roof. Climb up and take the Lamp, and once you have it tucked into your robe you shall be free of the garden and of the golden chambers. Wander where you will, take what you like, but be sure to bring the Lamp and everything back to me here at the top of the stairs.

"Go now, and for fear that any harm befalls you before you get to the Lamp take this ring, which will serve as protection so long as you keep to all that I have said," and the magician drew from off his finger his seal-ring and gave it to Aladdin.

Aladdin lowered himself down the hole until his feet reached the top step of the stairs and then he set off to follow all the directions his uncle had given him. Everything was there: the four chambers with their pots of gold, the doorway into the garden, the pathway through the trees, and the Lamp, hanging over the ladder. So Aladdin climbed up the thirty

* cubit: measurement (length of a forearm)

rungs, unhooked the Lamp from its gimbal*, stuffed it into his robe, climbed down the thirty rungs and set off to explore the garden.

What his uncle said was true. There could surely be no other garden like this one. The grass was greener and smoother than anywhere else, the water was bluer than anywhere else, the flowers were piled up in colours more variegated than anywhere else, and as for the trees – Aladdin more or less choked. Every tree was not just more shapely than any tree he'd ever seen, but every tree also had, dangling from its branches, great clusters of glittering fruit of bewildering brilliance. Now if Aladdin had spent more time at study, or working with the merchants of the bazaar, he would have realised straightway that this fruit was not just any sort of glass bauble and crystal, but was nothing less than rare gemstones: emeralds and diamonds, rubies, spinels and balasses of a size and perfection that was ridiculous. Such things could not be possible. But Aladdin was very taken with them, so he pulled down as big an assortment of them as he could and he stuffed them into his pockets and his turban and every fold of his clothing that could carry them, and he made his way back to the staircase, rattling like a bag of marbles. He was so weighed down with the things that there was no hope of him taking any gold from the great jars on the marble tables.

By the time he got back to the top of the stairs his uncle was pretty cross, what with hanging about up there most of the afternoon waiting for Aladdin to finish his fruit-picking. "Come on, then," he said,

* gimbal: a pivoted mount for keeping instruments level

sharpish, when Aladdin got on to the top step, "give us the Lamp and then I'll help you climb out."

Well, it was true that Aladdin needed some help: for one thing it was a big pull up out of the cave, and for another he was so weighed down with all his winnings that he was bothered how he could clamber up on his own, but he didn't see any point in passing the Lamp out first, especially since it was lodged round his belly somewhere, submerged under all the gemstones.

"Oh, no, Uncle, don't worry about that. Just give us a hand and then I'll find it for you."

"Oh, no, Nephew. Lamp first, then I'll give you a hand."

"But that's daft," said Aladdin, and went on arguing the toss until gradually he came to realize that there was more to this Lamp than he thought. His uncle obviously didn't want it just to read in bed with (and that was true, as we shall see). In the end the magician lost his head with fury and frustration.

"Damn you to hell!" he cried, "*zambahshala-mahzarúska!*" and with that wild and magical imprecation* he caused the marble slab to fall back over the hole with a crash, nearly smashing in Aladdin's skull as it did so.

There he was, shut in the dark, while the Moorish magician tramped off down the valley and took his way back to Africa as quick as he could.

The Lamp
Aladdin was now in a right fix. He tried yelling to see if the man would let him out, but by this time he'd

* imprecation: curse

worked out that the wizard fellow was no uncle of his and that he was the victim of some mysterious plot, so he didn't have much hope of seeing daylight soon in that direction. But nor did he have any luck in the other direction either. With the crashing shut of the trapdoor, the doors to all the chambers and the garden crashed shut too, and Aladdin was hemmed in on his staircase in total darkness.

"Truly there is no God but The God," said Aladdin, "He sends us mirth and He sends us misery. Alhamdohlillah; praise to the All-knowing, the Omnipotent, and to his Prophet Mohammed." And as he prayed these prayings he lifted his arms into the darkness, lowered them, and brought his hands together in supplication over the gemstones, rattling about in his robe.

Now as he sat there, moving his hands in prayer, it so happened that the fingers of one hand rubbed against the ring which the magician had given him when he first set off into the cave. And as he rubbed the ring, so there leapt forth in a shower of bright sparks an Ifrit from the tribe of the Jann of Solomon (for Aladdin's ring was one of those blessed with power by the great king). "Speak!" cried the Jinni. "I am the Slave of the Ring! Speak and tell me your desires!"

Well, Aladdin was flabbergasted; one minute locked in a pitch-black dungeon for good, the next minute asked to give orders – he didn't well know what to do. But after goggling for a bit at the Jinni he realized that this was the best chance he had of getting away, so he said, "Slave of the Ring, get me out of here."

Whoosh! He'd hardly blinked when he found

himself sitting on the ground above the entrance to the cavern, now all tidied over and hidden again. The Jinni had disappeared and Aladdin decided there was nothing for it but to walk back home and try to recover his wits a little. So he trudged off down the valley, and past the gardens, and into the town, with all his treasures still rattling and rolling round in his pockets and his turban and under his robe.

"Well, what happened to you?" asked his mother when he got home, "and what's become of Uncle?"

"Don't ask me!" said Aladdin, "don't say a word!" and without more ado he went off to his room where he unloaded all his pockets and his undergarments into some empty jars, put the Lamp on a table, climbed into bed and went to sleep.

Next morning, first thing, he told his mum what had occurred with his uncle. "Allah protect us!" said Mrs Tuanki, "what are we to do now? No sooner does someone come along to get you out of the gutter, teach you some manners, fix you up in a respectable job, give us some housekeeping-money, than you go and offend him so that he won't come back. That puts me back at my spinning and how we shall make out I just don't know."

"Now stop fashing*," said Aladdin, "and we'll sort something out. First off, you may like to know that I brought a few things back from out of that cave, and they should see us through for a while. Look at this old Lamp, for instance," fetching the Lamp out of his room, "we could polish that up for a start and we'd get a bob or two for it down at the market."

Well, that seemed quite a good idea, so his mum

* fashing: worrying

fetched out the lamp-cleaning stuff and Aladdin set to work to fettle it up. But no sooner had he started to polish it than there was another great flash and out came a Jinni three times bigger and three times meaner than the last one. "Speak!" he roared, so that poor Mrs Tuanki got all her spinning in a tangle. "I am the Slave of the Lamp and of all who hold the Lamp; command me and all my fellows to whatever you desire!"

This time Aladdin was beginning to get the hang of Jann and he answered, "Breakfast. Breakfast for two – the best you can manage", and in half a shake of a donkey's tail the Jinni was back with a gigantic silver tray. All down both sides of the tray there were twelve golden bowls, steaming with good things, and in the middle there were two silver goblets and two leather bottles full of old wine. "By heck," said Aladdin, "I'm ready for this," and as the Jinni vanished he went and untangled his mother, and the two of them set about their meal.

Now Aladdin's mum was not very keen on tinkering with supernatural forces, and as soon as she'd finished her breakfast she started trying to persuade Aladdin to have no more to do with them. "Take that ring and that Lamp," she said, "and throw them in the river." But Aladdin would have none of it. For one thing he thought he might get breakfasts like that every day of the week, and for another he realized that all the shenanigans with his so-called uncle had been because of the Lamp. If the chap was willing to go through all that plotting to try to get hold of it, then it must be a pretty powerful instrument.

Anyway, to keep his mother happy he decided that

he wouldn't call on the Slave more than he had to. Instead he settled to try to get by more comfortably by selling off, one by one, the bowls and the goblets that the Jinni had brought. When the money was used up from selling one he'd sell the next. At first the merchants in the bazaar thought that he was an easy pushover – probably fencing stolen goods any- way – but he gradually came to see the value of the stuff that he was bargaining with and before long he turned into a shrewd dealer. What's more, when the goods ran out he could always call up the Slave of the Lamp and order some more.

The Princess
Everything would have gone on nicely from this time forward, except that one day Aladdin was going down to the market when he heard a great racket. The Sultan's men were coming, and with them the Town Crier who was yelling, "Beware, beware! By order of the Sultan, Lord of the Time and Master of the Age, let all men leave the streets and markets and immure them in their houses; for the daughter of the Sultan, the Princess Badr al-Budur, now comes this way in train for the hammam baths. Let no man be present, upon pain of death, to see the Princess as she passes!"

Well, that was enough for Aladdin. He'd long heard of the beauty and grace of the Princess, and he'd not been shut up in caves and magicked by wizards without reckoning that he could take a look at a Princess if he wanted to. So he went to the hammam baths and he found a little cranny, at the back of the door, where he could creep in and see the Princess as she came.

Sheesh! For once the newsmongers had got it wrong in the wrong direction. Not all the reports of the Princess's beauty had quite prepared Aladdin for the revelation of her face and form as she passed by his little hidey-hole. His knees went weak with love for her and he almost fell out of concealment – which would have been the worse for him. Anyway, from that day forth there was nothing for it but he must sort out a way to marry her.

What he did was this: first of all he persuaded his mum that she was going to have to make his proposal for him. (She thought he was downright crackers, and decided that they'd both end up getting their heads chopped off, but by this time Aladdin was a pretty determined character and she had learnt to do as he told her.) Then he went into his room and began to sort out some of the fanciest jewels from those that he'd found in the cave. "Now let's have a bowl," he said to his mum, and she hunted around the house, but the best she could come up with was her big baking-bowl out of the kitchen. "That'll do nicely," said Aladdin, and he piled in the jewels, which seemed to glitter and shine all the more brilliantly for their plain setting; and he covered the lot with a blue-check table-cloth.

"Now," says Aladdin, "what I want you to do is to take this lot down to the Sultan's palace and get in the queue for the audience-chamber. They should let you in sometime this morning and you wait in there till someone calls you up to see the Sultan. Then you give him this bowl and say something on the lines of, 'Oh my Lord, may the blessings of Allah be upon you, my son back home wants to marry your daughter and he's sent this stuff as a courting-present ... ' and so on, and so forth. That should make him think."

"By gow!" says his mum, "make him think! It'll do more than that. It'll make him send for his Sworder there and then, and they'll have my head rolling on the floor before you can say 'Jack Robinson'!"

"All right, all right," says Aladdin, "I can see that it all looks a bit dodgy – but believe you me, it'll work out all right."

There was nothing she could say any more to persuade him, so she picked up the bowl and made her way down to the palace just as she was, in her moth-eaten widow's weeds.

When she got there, everything happened as Aladdin had predicted – except that she hung around in the audience-chamber all day and nobody took any notice of her. The Sultan did all the Sultan-ish things that he was there for, but the Wazirs and the chamberlains and the vergers paid no heed to the little old woman all in black with her baking-bowl.

The same thing happened the next day, and the next day, and the next, all the same for about a month, till Aladdin began to get a bit vexed. "What're you doing?" he said, "you're not trying. You must just be a bit more pushy."

Equally though, the Sultan was beginning to get more and more curious about this shabby, silent figure who kept turning up day by day. "Who is she?" he asked the Grand Wazir, "what does she want? If she's here tomorrow see that she's called before me."

Accordingly, next day, no one was more surprised, or flustered, than Mrs Tuanki when she was called up to the Sultan first off. "Oh my Lord," she said, kissing the ground in front of him, "Oh my Lord,

Allah bless thee, and Allah forgive me, but I have a boon to ask which is for thine ears only. Hear me, and then too grant me forgiveness."

"Very well," said the Sultan, "if it's something that Allah can forgive then I'm sure I can too," and turning to the Grand Wazir he said, "Clear the court!"

Grumbling mightily the folk in the audience-chamber were cleared back to the street; the courtiers went out, and Aladdin's mum was left confronting the Sultan and the Grand Wazir who stayed as his chief adviser. "So what's all the fuss about?" asked the Sultan, and Aladdin's mum entered into the whole story about how Aladdin was wasting away for love of the Sultan's daughter and had sent her along to ask for her hand in marriage.

The Sultan was so astounded by the cheek of this proposal, coming from such a decrepit old woman, that the only thing he could do was laugh. "In the name of Allah," he cried, "we are a noble nation that even a tailor's widow may seek a Princess for a daughter-in-law – and I suppose that's your wedding present in there," pointing to the baking-bowl.

"Well as it happens, my Lord, it is," said Mrs Tuanki, much relieved that the Sultan was taking everything so matily, and she pulled the blue-check cloth off the baking-bowl. Wow! Red, green, blue, silver, gold, the jewels shone out with amazing radiance, turning the audience-chamber into a gallery that danced with colour. Aladdin's mum (who hadn't been expecting anything quite like that) fell over backwards with surprise and the Sultan and his Grand Wazir leapt out of their chairs for fear the whole brilliant vessel might there and then explode.

"Madam," said the Sultan, when he'd come back to his senses, "Madam; allow me to pay mind to this present of yours," and he began to examine the contents of the bowl with some care, picking out gems of especial magnificence and seeing, with a practised eye, that this baking-bowl held more treasure than the treasury of his own palace. Plainly the son of this decrepit widow was a person to be reckoned with, and if he had more jewels where these came from, he would make a match for the Princess Badr al-Budur beyond that of any other suitor.

That was the trouble, though. For before Mrs Tuanki ever appeared on the scene the Sultan's Grand Wazir had made approaches to his Lord in the interests of his son, and it was all but settled that this young chap was going to marry the Princess – thus keeping all the monkeys together at the top of the tree. But the Wazir's son was not likely to come up with courting-presents like Aladdin's and the Sultan was bothered to know how he could keep his Wazir happy and get his hands on the jewellery.

"Madam," he said again (can't you just hear him!) "we are honoured to be seen as worthy to receive a gift of this ethereal splendour, and honoured that the giver should think so highly of us that he seeks the hand of our daughter in marriage. How could we refuse? But I fear that we cannot accede to your request with absolute spontaneity, for you must know that the Princess Badr al-Budur is just now engaged in a religious retreat, and nothing can be done until her return in three months' time. Pray tell your son, the honourable Messire Aladdin, that we shall convey the treasure of his heart and of his house to our daughter and shall await a prosperous engagement when our daughter shall return."

Bridegroom Number One
"I don't like it," said Mrs Tuanki when she got back home. "He's given us the brush-off and he's kept all those jewels. What was all that about a religious retreat? First time I ever heard of Princesses doing a thing like that... " But Aladdin didn't seem to mind. "You told him," he said; "you gave him the present. He knows what's what. We'll just wait and see what happens." So wait they did.

But although the Sultan had said what he said in order to gain time, he'd reckoned without the persistence of the Grand Wazir. That one wasn't going to see his son lose out to some inconsequential peasant. So he kept on at the Sultan (he was good at keeping on, that was one of the things he was paid for), and so it turned out that the Sultan began to think that the bowlful of jewels was a simple piece of good fortune and that his daughter really ought to marry the Wazir's son. Why not? It had always seemed a good idea. Let's get on with it.

So one day, a couple of months after her audience with the Sultan, Aladdin's mum went down to the town and was startled to see flags flying and bunting in the streets. "What's going on here, then?" she asked; and they told her that the Wazir's son was getting betrothed to the Sultan's daughter.

"Where've you been then, missus?" they said. "Haven't you heard about that already?"

Without more ado, Mrs Tuanki went back to Aladdin and told him the news. "I never did trust those folk," he said, "but don't you mind. I've not

102

done with them yet," and he sat quietly at home while everyone in town got drunk. That evening, when they'd all gone to bed, he went into his room and rubbed the Lamp. Flash! there was the Jinni. "I am the Slave of the Lamp!" he roared, "and of all who hold the Lamp; command me and all my fellows to whatever you desire. Speak!" So Aladdin spoke and told him what he was to do: he was to go and fetch the Princess Badr al-Budur and the Wazir's son on their bridal couch, he was to dump the Wazir's son in the marsh out back and keep guard over him for the night, then in the morning he was to take them and the couch back to the Sultan's palace.

All this the Jinni accomplished. Aladdin spent the night moonstruck by the sleeping Princess, the Wazir's son spent the night getting cold cramps in the bog, and next day they found themselves back at the palace in time for breakfast. "Well that was a funny dream," said the Princess, and told her mum what had happened; but the Wazir's son sat shivering and said nothing at all.

Next night the same thing happened. The Princess and the Wazir's son had hardly got to bed before the Jinni came again and dumped the boy in the bog and the girl in the room in front of Aladdin's adoring gaze. Then back to the palace for breakfast. This time the Wazir's son spoke up. "I've had enough of this," he said, "if it's someone's idea of a joke they can try it on another muggins in the future," and he went back home and refused to go on with the marriage. The Grand Wazir did all he could to persuade him to change his mind – because, after all, the Princess Badr al-Budur was a pretty good catch – but the lad was so clemmed with the damp-cold and so frightened of the Jinni that he decided the Heavens were against the whole match.

As for the Princess, she still thought that it had all been a dream – but not by any means as offensive as the Wazir's son made out.

Bridegroom Number Two
With all the excitement over the wedding and everything that happened after, the Sultan had quite forgotten his promise to Aladdin's mother. But of course she'd not forgotten – nor Aladdin neither – and when the three months were up from the day she'd handed over the jewels, she went back to the audience-chamber in the Palace and waited to see the Sultan.

This time though, she didn't have to wait long. No sooner did the Sultan see this little bitty woman in her raggety gown than he remembered what had happened and he called over his Grand Wazir for a hasty confabulation. "Look who's there," he whispered, "you know what she's come for. What are we going to do about that?"

Now the Grand Wazir was still sore about his son backing out of the marriage, and he certainly wasn't keen for anyone else to step in – least of all these people. "Easy, my Lord," he said, "all you have to do is ask for more dowry. Tell her that everything can be arranged but that you'll need – er – hem – um" (counting on his fingers), "forty more bowls of jewellery like the last lot. That should settle her."

So the Sultan called up Mrs Widow Tuanki, who straightway reminded him that this was the end of the three-month interval and hoped that his daughter was now finished with the religious retreat, being as how she should now be set to marry Aladdin. "Indeed, indeed, dear Madam," said the Sultan, "did you think we had forgotten? Why, all is now ready to be set in train – processions, ceremonies, feasts and so forth – and all we need is the rest of the dower-gifts."

"Eh?" said Aladdin's mum, "dower-gifts? That's the first I've heard of those. What does your Excellency have in mind?"

Well, the Sultan got the Grand Wazir to explain about the forty bowls of gemstones, and that gentleman threw in for good measure that they expected delivery to be made by forty dancing girls, escorted by forty body slaves, and all by tomorrow afternoon, if you please. What's more, he hoped the weather would keep fine for the wedding.

Aladdin's mum returned home all cast down. She didn't really understand how her boy had come by all those jewels in the first place, and she certainly didn't see how he could get any more – but she gave him the message none the less. "Fine," said Aladdin, "let's get on with it"; and he straightway went off to his room, rubbed the Lamp, and told the Jinni what had happened and what they had to do.

"I hear and obey, Master," said the Jinni, and before Mrs Tuanki could think straight there started up a grand procession from her house to the Sultan's palace: forty dancing girls, each carrying an earthenware bowl of gems from the hoard in the garden, and each protected by a slave, walking beside her with a drawn scimitar. And very lovely they all looked too.

"Go on, Mum," said Aladdin, "go on with them. Give my best respects to the Sultan and tell him that

I'll be along to marry the Princess in the morning – while the weather holds."

And so it came about. The Sultan and the Grand Wazir were just finishing the last of the day's business in the audience-chamber when they heard a great racket outside and in walked Aladdin's mum, still in her old robe, followed by the dancing girls with all the trinkets. The hall shone with their brightness, and Mrs Tuanki kneeled before the Sultan and said, "The wedding gifts, my Lord. My son Aladdin will be here tomorrow."

The Sultan was thunderstruck. The Grand Wazir turned green with rage. But there was nothing for it. What they'd asked for, they'd got, and for the second time that season they had to set about fixing a wedding for the Princess Badr al-Budur. (She, of course, didn't have any say in the matter, but she was glad enough to get away from the Wazir's son, whom she'd always thought was a bit of a weed, and she didn't think there could be much wrong with a newcomer who gave her bowlfuls of jewels for a present.)

The flags and the bunting were brought out again, and the next morning Aladdin set out in state to make himself known to his future father-in-law. He had called up the Slave of the Lamp before he left and this was the order of his train:

twenty-four Mamelukes with war-chargers and
accoutrements;
Aladdin
on a white stallion, whose saddle and bridle were
encrusted with gems;
twelve more Mamelukes with war-chargers and

106

accoutrements;
forty-eight white slaves,
each carrying a bowl in which were a thousand
gold pieces;
Aladdin's mum;
twelve handmaids clothed as the daughters of
morning,
and all surrounded by a guard of honour,
crying:
"Praise to Allah! Praise to Him who Changeth and
is not Changed!"

Admittedly it looked a bit like an army, but Aladdin had various of the Mamelukes and the slaves throw gold pieces in among the crowd as they travelled along the streets, so everybody blessed him for a proper gentleman, just right for their Princess.

When the procession eventually reached the Sultan's palace, Aladdin rode to the front and greeted him with a pretty speech thanking the Sultan for agreeing to bestow his daughter on so humble a person … not being worthy of so precious a jewel … tongue-tied by so much honour … etc., etc., until the Sultan thought it best to interrupt and suggest that they all went indoors for a cup of tea. This they did, and in the course of their further conversation Aladdin happened to remark that he was eager to build a little house or pavilion which might serve as a new home for his bride, and did the Sultan have any thoughts on the matter?

"Well," said the Sultan, "it so happens that there's a stretch of land opposite my palace there which we only use for practising polo on, why don't you build something there?"

"Very well then," said Aladdin, "I'll get that done,

and then we can proceed with the wedding and so on," and with much bowing and arm-waving he left the room and took himself off to a quiet place. Here he pulled the Lamp from out of his wedding robes, rubbed it, and out sprang the Slave of the Lamp: "Speak, Lord! Command me and my fellows to whatever you may desire!" and Aladdin thereupon ordered the building of a pavilion that might be one of the wonders of the world:

Its outer stones were of jasper and alabaster, inlaid with marble and mosaic-work; within were chambers within chambers, each furnished to perfection, and containing proper stores of household utensils, and wardrobes of fine robes, and chests full of gold and silverware and caskets of bright gems; and there were kitchens and stables, all serviced with attendants and slaves, and over all there was a great belvedere*, looking out over town and country, with twenty-four windows decorated with emeralds and rubies – except at one corner, and there, there was only plain plasterwork – unfinished.

All this Aladdin commanded, and in a trice it was done; whereupon Aladdin asked the Jinni to lay a carpet of gold-inwrought brocade from the door of his pavilion to the entrance of the Sultan's palace. Then he returned to the company and invited them to come and see the little house that he'd put up for his bride.

Well – between you and me – up till now they'd treated Aladdin as a bit of a joke. After all, he'd never tried to hide the fact that he was a tailor's son, and they all thought that he'd struck it lucky somehow

* belvedere: raised turret on roof

or other but that it wouldn't last. When they came to the door of the palace though, and saw that gleaming new building rising up beyond the courtyard they were astounded.

"Wonderful … gorgeous … majestic," they all said to each other, but the Grand Wazir said, "Sorcery! We are all at the mercy of the Prince of Darkness!"

"Well, we all know what you mean by that," said the Sultan, "you're still jealous because Aladdin's marrying my daughter instead of your son. Come on, let's go and look at this sorcery."

So with the Sultan in the lead they all trooped along the golden carpet to the door of the pavilion, where Aladdin formally greeted them and bade them welcome. Then he took the Sultan round the rooms of the house, disclosing all their comforts and treasures. Eventually they climbed to the belvedere with its sights across land and sea, and as the Sultan was marvelling at the opulence of it all, so he came to the window set in unadorned plaster. "Ho!" he said, "what of this then? Your builder seems to have missed a bit out."

"Too true," said Aladdin, "too true. But such was the speed that we worked, to please your Highness and the daughter of your Highness, we didn't have time to finish the building before your visit. It shall be done tomorrow."

"There you are then," said the Sultan, looking at the Grand Wazir, "what sort of sorcery is that if it can't finish the job properly? You impugn my son-in-law too readily." And he ordered his own architect and his own builders to complete the work on the window and gave signal for the festivities to begin, to celebrate the marriage of Aladdin to the Princess Badr al-Budur.

The Wizard

From that day on there seemed to be nothing that could spoil the good fortune and the happiness of Aladdin and his family. The Princess discovered that she liked her new husband even more than she liked the jewels that he kept producing; Aladdin's mum found housekeeping in the royal pavilion a good deal more agreeable than spinning in the back streets; and Aladdin himself struck up a chummy relationship with the Sultan and they used to go hunting and fishing and playing polo together when the Sultan wasn't having to give audiences and suchlike.

But we've forgotten about that Moorish magician who was the cause of all this in the first place (and that's not surprising, because Aladdin had forgotten about him too). Over in Africa though, the magician had not forgotten about Aladdin. He hadn't been home long before he began to be sorry that he'd lost his temper when he shut Aladdin in the cave – especially since he'd shut his Ring of Solomon in there too – and he began to ponder how he might make good some of his losses.

He got out all his sand-tables and stuff and he began to make some prognostications about what might be happening in China – and you can guess his surprise when he discovered that Aladdin was not only still alive but was now Master of the Slave of the Lamp. He just about had a fit.

"Exterminate him; exterminate him!" he yelled, stamping round the room and kicking his apparatus,

"I shall not rest till I have encompassed his destruction."

Straightway he began to make his plans, and once again he set off for China. This time he had no need to comb the streets for his victim, because everyone was still talking about the Emir Aladdin, his pavilion of splendour, and his habit of throwing golden dinars around whenever he went for a walk. Indeed, you could see the belvedere of the pavilion, with its (now) twenty-four glittering windows, from every side of the town, and the wizard need only do a few simple spells with his sand-table to discover that the Lamp of Power was kept in the house and not carried about by Aladdin wherever he went.

"That has him," said the magician, and he set about obtaining a stock of brand-new copper lamps which he carefully packed in baskets for loading on to a donkey. When all was ready he waited till he heard news that Aladdin had gone out hunting, and then he started through the town like any trader in the streets. "New lamps!" he cried. "New lamps for old! Come on, ladies, do yourselves a favour, out with your old lamps; every old lamp gets a new one in exchange! Roll up, roll up! New lamps for old!"

Well, it wasn't long before half the city was following along behind him, pointing their fingers at him and calling everyone else to watch. "He's barmy," they shouted, "look at old barmy-boots! Go fetch your old lamps and get him to give you a new one!"

Before long the wizard made sure that he was in the street going past Aladdin's house, and with all the commotion, the Princess Badr al-Budur couldn't help sending to know if it was bloody revolution or what-all. "Oh, ma'am," said the servant coming back, "it's a mad African, giving away new lamps in exchange for old ones. Everyone's laughing at him. But – come to think of it – the Master's got a dirty old lamp, stuck away in his back room, let's swap it and give him a surprise." Which is just what they did. They sent a slave down to the street to change Aladdin's old lamp for a new one and as soon as he'd done so the magician discerned that the Lamp of Power was now in his hands. "Take the lot, you idiots! Take the lot!" he cried, and he tipped the donkey-baskets all over the road, and while everyone rushed up to see what they could find he made off into the side streets round the back.

When he'd got clear of the crowds and into a deserted part of the town, the wizard sat down to wait for nightfall, and then he rubbed the Lamp. Shezam! out came the Jinni. "Speak! I am the Slave of the Lamp; command me and all my fellows to whatever you desire!"

"Well, it's good to meet you after all this time," said the wizard, "here's what I want," and he commanded the Slave of the Lamp to uproot Aladdin's pavilion and all that was in it and to carry the lot (with the magician included) back to his estates in Africa. "Hearing and obeying!" said the Jinni, and straightway the whole caboodle was magicked off to Africa, leaving nothing but the polo practice-ground in front of the Sultan's palace.

In the morning, when he woke up, the Sultan did what he usually did and drew the curtains to look across at Aladdin's pavilion. And there it was – gone. He closed his eyes, and opened them again slowly.

Still gone. So he sent for the Grand Wazir. "What's happened then?" he asked.

"Wha'd'you mean 'what's happened then?'" asked the Wazir, who'd only just woken up.

"Where is it?" asked the Sultan.

"Where's what?" asked the Wazir.

"That," said the Sultan, and he pointed out of the window.

The Wazir gulped. "Well, it was there last night… and… and… oh! Excellency," (wringing his hands) "isn't that what I've said all along? It's sorcery. We've all been duped by sorcerers!"

This time the Sultan was more inclined to believe his Grand Wazir – especially since he'd now lost his daughter – but it wasn't long before he discovered that Aladdin hadn't been in the pavilion but had gone off hunting.

"Very well," he said, "he must be arrested. Guards!… " and he called up the captain of the guard and ordered him to go and hunt Aladdin and to bring him back a prisoner. The fellow was a sorcerer and would have his head chopped off.

The captain of the guard was surprised about this because, like everyone else, he'd always found the Emir Aladdin a sociable sort of chap, as unsorcerer-like as they come. But Sultan's orders were Sultan's orders, so he took his men into the forest and before long they'd found Aladdin and taken him back to the palace, a prisoner. He marched up to the Sultan's room: tramp, tramp, tramp! "Now," said the Sultan, "what's the meaning of this?" and he pointed out of the window to where Aladdin's pavilion wasn't. Aladdin looked and, like the Sultan and Wazir before him, looked again. Polo practice-ground; nothing else.

"Your Highness," said Aladdin, "I don't know. To be sure, everything was there when I went away, how should I know what's become of it?"

"Well, it's your house," said the Sultan, "you ought to look after it; and that thing on your neck is your head, and you ought to look after that too. If you can't find your house and my daughter in the next six months I'll have it put on a pole by the city gate."

"Six months," cried Aladdin, "six months! Good grief! If I can't find them all in the next six weeks I'll chop my head off myself and bring it to you as a present."

So they let Aladdin go and he began to wander round in a disconsolate sort of way, pondering how a place that size could have vanished and how he could set about finding it. And as it turned out, his ramblings led him to the self-same valley where he'd had the adventure with the treasure cave and that suddenly reminded him about his Ring, blessed with the power of Solomon himself. So without more ado he rubbed the Ring, there on his finger, and out came the Jinni: "Speak! I am the Slave of the Ring; speak and tell me your desires!"

"Slave of the Ring," said Aladdin, "my house is vanished, my wife is vanished, find them and bring them back to the place of their proper abode."

"Alas!" said the Jinni, "that may not be. These things are beyond my competence, for they are now in the power of the Slave of the Lamp. I dare not attempt it."

"Very well," said Aladdin, "in that case take me to my house."

"I hear and obey," said the Jinni, and in the space of an eye-glance he set Aladdin down beside his pavilion in Africa. There he was, just under the window of the Princess Badr al-Budur.

Hardly had Aladdin staggered to his feet and settled that this was, indeed, his house when the Princess's window opened and the Princess's maidservant put her head out to get some fresh air. She spotted this Chinese-looking chap down below and nearly fell out of the window as she recognized Aladdin. "O my lady! O my lady!" she called back into the room, "here's my Lord Aladdin standing in the garden!" The Princess rushed up to the window, and when she saw that it certainly was Aladdin, she threw down one of her bracelets from her wrist so that he looked up at her. "Round the back!" she called at him in a sort of whisper. "Go through the little door round the back!" and she sent the maidservant down to bring Aladdin to her room.

Apparently the wizard was at that time doing some shopping in an African city down the road, so Aladdin and the Princess Badr al-Budur were able to have a long talk about the peculiar things that had happened. "Tell me," said Aladdin, by way of a start, "have you come across an old copper lamp that I used to keep round at the back of my room?"

"Oh," said the Princess, "don't talk about that. We took it down to the street to a hawker who was swapping old lamps for new ones, and now it's got into the hands of the Maghrabi – the Accursed One – who brought us here, and he treasures it as the source of all Power. He carries it about with him all the time, tucked down the inside of his robe."

When he heard that, Aladdin understood everything,

and saw what now had to be done. It seemed that ever since they'd made their instantaneous journey to Africa, the Princess and the magician had been at daggers drawn, because he would keep on trying to persuade her that Aladdin was dead and she'd best marry him and have done with it, while she reckoned she knew different and wasn't going to have any truck with a trickster anyway.

What Aladdin now suggested was that she should appear to change her mind – give up on the idea that her man was still alive and offer a bit of encouragement to the wizard. Then, if she could inveigle him into having a drink with her, she could spike his liquor and they'd have a fair chance of getting back the Lamp. And Aladdin went off to where his old room used to be, dug around in a cabinet and came back with a couple of white pills. "Crush those up and put them in his glass," he said, "they'll do the trick."

And that's what happened. When the wizard came back from the shops Aladdin hid behind a curtain and the Princess Badr al-Budur got herself up to look all sexy. "Why don't you come up and see me some time this evening?" she said to the magician, "I'm tired of being cooped up here all on my own; I could do with some company."

Well, a nod's as good as a wink to a blind man, so they say, and the wizard was quite taken in by this apparent change of heart. (He'd always had a high opinion of himself, and couldn't see why the Princess hadn't fallen for him first off anyway.) So that evening he smartened himself up and came up to the Princess's apartments for some supper, while the

Princess, for her part, made sure that everything was comfy and there was plenty to drink.

Oh dear, you fellows who are listening to this story, let it be a lesson to you all. She waggled her hips at the old chap, in her silken trousers; she flashed her eyes at him over her flimsy veil – and she kept on pouring. From a state of delight, to a state of euphoria, he went on tipping back his glass until he was eventually almost catatonic* and could hardly have got his hands on her if he'd tried. Then it was that she slipped the crushed powder into his drink and he keeled over for good.

Out from behind the curtain came Aladdin, with a dagger in his hand. They fished around inside the wizard's robe till they found where he'd tucked away the Lamp, and when they'd got it out and made sure it was the right one, Aladdin shoved the dagger into his ribs and put an end to his wizardry forever.

How It Ended

You might think that there's not much more to be said. You might think that all we need to do is to tell how Aladdin once more summoned the Slave of the Lamp, ordered him to take the house back to where it started from, and how the Sultan – waking up next morning – was as surprised to see the pavilion back on the polo-ground as he had been to see it vanished. Obviously he was delighted to have his daughter home again, and was all ready to forgive and forget – so you might think that they all lived happily ever after. But you'd be wrong.

You see the African magician had a brother, who

* catatonic: paralytic

was a pretty good wizard on his own account. They never saw much of each other, but they liked to keep in touch at Christmas, as it were, and the brother began to get a bit agitated when the usual greetings never turned up. So he got his own set of sand-tables and magical instruments and he did a bit of conjuring – and what did he discover but that his brother had been murdered and his body carried off to China, to the city of all cities.

"Vengeance is mine," said Wizard Number Two – or words to that effect – and he straightway set out for China to see what he could do about it. He travelled long weeks and months over the seas and the mountains and finally ended up outside the city in what was called 'the Strangers' Khan', a kind of hostelry for foreigners. Here he began his investigations to find out more about his brother's murderer and ways to get at him, and he had the good fortune one day to hear some dominoes players in a nearby tavern talking about the Holy Fatimah. Apparently this Holy Fatimah was a saintly hermitess from the mountains, who'd been causing quite a stir lately with various acts of piety and healing, and she was due to be coming to town soon to bless, and be blessed by, the Sultan and his family. So the wizard found out where she lived – up in a little cave above the city – and set off to visit her.

He arrived at the cave, as he'd planned, round about night-time and he waited on guard there until early next morning, when he went inside and found the hermitess just waking up. Before she could say anything he pulled out his dagger and forced her there and then to change clothes with him, or else … When he'd done that he made her fetch her staff and her other gear and he got her to show him how she went about her ministrations – and when he'd done that, and got it all off pat, he asked her for a rope for a girdle, and that he used to hang her with. Just like that. He hanged her there in the cave and then threw her body into a nearby pit. So much for wizards ...

Once he'd got rid of the Holy Fatimah he went down to the city in her cloak, and with her veil covering his beard and his mustachios, and he made for the Sultan's palace. Before he got there though, there was so much commotion, with everybody in the street wanting a benediction or a Touch, that he attracted the attention of the Princess Badr al-Budur, who asked her maid to bring him straight into the house.

This, of course, was just what he wanted. Imitating the Holy Fatimah he behaved all smarmy (said he wouldn't take anything to eat because he was fasting, but really because he was worried about someone seeing his whiskers), and he let her show him around the pavilion. Everywhere they went he gave the right sort of gasps of astonishment, but when at last they got to the belvedere on the roof he allowed himself a sigh of disappointment. "Oh, dear!" he said, "such a beautiful room, but spoiled for want of a last perfection."

"What do you mean?" asked the Princess, "'spoiled for want of a last perfection'; what could possibly make the place more perfect?"

"Ah," said the Fatimah Wizard, "what you need here – right in the middle of the ceiling – is a Rukh's egg. They're not easy to come by. They belong to the largest birds in the world. But a Rukh's egg, hanging there from the middle of the ceiling ... perfect!"

Well, the Princess Badr al-Budur was pretty upset about this, and after she'd sent Fatimah off to have a rest before meeting the Sultan, she sent for Aladdin. "What's the trouble?" says he.

"Duff!" says she. "A duff job. You set about building the smartest place in the kingdom and you don't finish it off properly. Where's the Rukh's egg that ought to be hanging from the ceiling?" and she explained to him about the visit from Fatimah and what the old girl had said.

"Don't worry!" said Aladdin. "If it wasn't done then it can surely be done now," and he went off to his room, got out the Lamp and rubbed it. Flash! back came the Jinni. "Speak! I am the Slave of the Lamp! Command me and all my fellows to whatever you desire!"

"Well," said Aladdin, "what I want you to do is to fetch me the egg of a bird called a Rukh and hang it from the dome of my belvedere."

"Zambahshalamahzaruska!" roared the Jinni, and Aladdin collapsed on to the floor, "what insolent ingratitude is this? Have not we Slaves of the Lamp done all your biddings? Furnished your processions? Filled your bowls with gold? Built your mansion – and carried it backwards and forwards over the earth? Was that not enough, that you must now ask us to fetch our Mistress of Heaven and hang her up in your pleasure-dome? By Allah, I am minded to turn you to ashes and scatter you to the twelve quarters of the wind. Command me no more such commands." And the Jinni went back into the Lamp.

When Aladdin had recovered a little, and got up off the floor, he began to ponder why the Holy Fatimah should have made this suggestion which had so nearly brought about their downfall. What could she know of Rukhs' eggs? More than that – what could she know of Jann who had this intimate relationship with Rukhs' eggs?

So when he went downstairs he told the Princess, his wife, that he'd like to see the Holy Fatimah because he'd suddenly come over all peculiar, with a bad headache (which was not too far from the truth). The Princess sent for the hermitess, who should have finished her rest by now, and when the Fatimah Wizard came into the room and saw Aladdin standing there, he realized that all his schemes were moving to success. He went over to Aladdin, feeling in his robe as though to bring out some charm against headaches, but really palming his own dagger. Aladdin watched him with his eyes well open, and as the Holy Lady raised her arm he grabbed it by the wrist, twisted, and, when the dagger fell to the floor... picked it up and drove it through the robes and into the heart of the Moorish Wizard.

"Yow!" yelled the Princess; "Screech!" yelled the Princess's servants; but Aladdin stuck his foot on Fatimah's chest, pulled out the dagger, and then tore away the veiling so that everyone could see the Holy Woman's beard and mustachios. "All thanks to Allah and the Rukh's egg," said Aladdin; and now that Wizard One and Wizard Two were both out of the way Aladdin, and Aladdin's wife, and Aladdin's mum, and the Sultan and all the population of the city of cities (except possibly the Grand Wazir), lived happily ever after.

THE TALE OF SHEHEREZADE

With the ending of this story of Aladdin the first
sunbeam touched the minarets of the Sultan's palace
and Sheherezade knew that for a thousand nights
and one night she had been winning the mind and
heart of the Shah Shahryar. Through all this time
she had loved him – had borne his three boy-children
– and through all this time at the request of her sister
Dunyazad she had told him story upon story. But
now, as the dawn broke, she silenced the pleas of
Dunyazad, rose to her feet and, kissing the ground
before the King, she said: "Lord of the time and of
the age, I am thy handmaid. For a thousand nights
and one night I have entertained thee with tales and
legends, jests and moral instances, and now I crave
a boon of thee!"

And the King said, "Ask, O Sheherezade, and it
shall be granted unto thee."

Whereupon she cried: "Bring me my children!"
And when the nurses and eunuchs had brought the
children before the King she said: "O King of the age,
these are thy children and I crave that thou release
me from the doom of thy judgement, that I may rear
them fittingly as they should be reared."

Then the King answered: "O Sheherezade, I
pardoned thee before the coming of these children
for I found thee to be most candid and most fair.

Allah bless thee all thy days and may He witness against me that I exempt thee from aught that can harm thee." And with these words he called for his Wazirs and Emirs and for the Officers of the Crown and decreed that there should be public feasting to celebrate the marriage of the Shah Shahryar to Sheherezade. And in like way his brother, the Shah Zaman, who had ever followed his actions, begged that he might marry Dunyazad, so thus it came about that, amid rejoicings which no storyteller may describe, the two brothers were united to the two sisters and they dwelt together in all peace and happiness until there came to them the Destroyer of Delights, the Sunderer of Societies and the Garnerer of Graveyards.

GLOSSARY

alabaster	semi-transparent stone
Allah	God of the Islamic religion
asrafi	golden coin
bastinado	beating of soles of feet with a stick
bazaar	market place
Caliph	Islamic spiritual leader
caravan	company of people travelling together
ebony	hard black wood
emir	chieftain
eunuch	special sort of slave
dinar	Arabian golden coin
hammam baths	Turkish steam baths
harem	group of women all married to the same man
Hind	a person of the Hindu religion
Ifrit (sometimes spelt **afreet**)	evil demon
jasper	quartz
Jinni (sometimes spelt **genie**)	spirit
khan	an inn
Koran	the sacred book of Islam
Mameluke	member of an army
minaret	turret of a mosque
Mohammed	the Prophet of Islam
necromancer	sorcerer

Rukh (sometimes spelt **Roc**)	giant bird
salaam	greeting, salute
scimitar	short curved sword
Shah	king
Sheikh	chieftain
Sultan	Islamic ruler
sweetmeat	confectionery, sweet
Wazir	minister, counsellor

ALSO IN

Heinemann
New Windmills

Founding Editors: Anne and Ian Serraillier

Chinua Achebe Things Fall Apart
Vivien Alcock The Cuckoo Sister; The Monster Garden;
The Trial of Anna Cotman; A Kind of Thief; Ghostly Companions
Margaret Atwood The Handmaid's Tale
Jane Austen Pride and Prejudice
J G Ballard Empire of the Sun
Nina Bawden The Witch's Daughter; A Handful of Thieves; Carrie's
War; The Robbers; Devil by the Sea; Kept in the Dark; The Finding;
Keeping Henry; Humbug; The Outside Child
Valerie Bierman No More School
Melvin Burgess An Angel for May
Ray Bradbury The Golden Apples of the Sun; The Illustrated Man
Betsy Byars The Midnight Fox; Goodbye, Chicken Little; The
Pinballs; The Not-Just-Anybody Family; The Eighteenth Emergency
Victor Canning The Runaways; Flight of the Grey Goose
Ann Coburn Welcome to the Real World
Hannah Cole Bring in the Spring
Jane Leslie Conly Racso and the Rats of NIMH
Robert Cormier We All Fall Down; Tunes for Bears to Dance to
Roald Dahl Danny, The Champion of the World; The Wonderful
Story of Henry Sugar; George's Marvellous Medicine; The BFG;
The Witches; Boy; Going Solo; Matilda
Anita Desai The Village by the Sea
Charles Dickens A Christmas Carol; Great Expectations;
Hard Times; Oliver Twist; A Charles Dickens Selection
Peter Dickinson Merlin Dreams
Berlie Doherty Granny was a Buffer Girl; Street Child
Roddy Doyle Paddy Clarke Ha Ha Ha
Gerald Durrell My Family and Other Animals
Anne Fine The Granny Project
Anne Frank The Diary of Anne Frank
Leon Garfield Six Apprentices; Six Shakespeare Stories;
Six More Shakespeare Stories
Jamila Gavin The Wheel of Surya
Adele Geras Snapshots of Paradise

Alan Gibbons Chicken
Graham Greene The Third Man and The Fallen Idol; Brighton Rock
Thomas Hardy The Withered Arm and Other Wessex Tales
L P Hartley The Go-Between
Ernest Hemmingway The Old Man and the Sea; A Farewell to Arms
Nigel Hinton Getting Free; Buddy; Buddy's Song
Anne Holm I Am David
Janni Howker Badger on the Barge; Isaac Campion; Martin Farrell
Jennifer Johnston Shadows on Our Skin
Toeckey Jones Go Well, Stay Well
Geraldine Kaye Comfort Herself; A Breath of Fresh Air
Clive King Me and My Million
Dick King-Smith The Sheep-Pig
Daniel Keyes Flowers for Algernon
Elizabeth Laird Red Sky in the Morning; Kiss the Dust
D H Lawrence The Fox and The Virgin and the Gypsy;
Selected Tales
Harper Lee To Kill a Mockingbird
Ursula Le Guin A Wizard of Earthsea
Julius Lester Basketball Game
C Day Lewis The Otterbury Incident
David Line Run for Your Life
Joan Lingard Across the Barricades; Into Exile; The Clearance;
The File on Fraulein Berg
Robin Lister The Odyssey
Penelope Lively The Ghost of Thomas Kempe
Jack London The Call of the Wild; White Fang
Bernard Mac Laverty Cal; The Best of Bernard Mac Laverty
Margaret Mahy The Haunting
Jan Mark Do You Read Me? (Eight Short Stories)
James Vance Marshall Walkabout
W Somerset Maughan The Kite and Other Stories
Ian McEwan The Daydreamer; A Child in Time
Pat Moon The Spying Game
Michael Morpurgo Waiting for Anya; My Friend Walter;
The War of Jenkins' Ear
Bill Naughton The Goalkeeper's Revenge
New Windmill A Charles Dickens Selection
New Windmill Book of Classic Short Stories
New Windmill Book of Nineteenth Century Short Stories

How many have you read?